INTO THE NIGER BEND

The Fitzroy Edition of

JULES VERNE

Edited by I. O. Evans

A FLOATING CITY
THE BEGUM'S FORTUNE
FIVE WEEKS IN A BALLOON
DROPPED FROM THE
　CLOUDS
THE SECRET OF THE ISLAND
MICHAEL STROGOFF
THE DEMON OF CAWNPORE
TIGERS AND TRAITORS
FROM THE EARTH TO THE
　MOON
ROUND THE MOON
INTO THE NIGER BEND
THE CITY IN THE SAHARA

Into the Niger Bend

Part One of
The Barsac Mission

by

JULES VERNE

★

Translated from the French by
I. O. EVANS
F.R.G.S.

ASSOCIATED BOOKSELLERS
WESTPORT   CONN

Copyright © 1960 in England by
Arco Publications

All rights reserved

Set in ten point Baskerville
Printed in England by Clarke, Doble & Brendon Ltd., Oakfield Press,
Cattedown, Plymouth

CONTENTS

INTRODUCTION		*page* 7
I	THE CENTRAL BANK BUSINESS	11
II	A JOURNEY OF INVESTIGATION	29
III	LORD BLAZON OF GLENOR	41
IV	AN ARTICLE FROM "L'ÉXPANSION FRANCAISE"	61
V	SECOND ARTICLE BY AMÉDÉE FLORENCE	76
VI	AMÉDÉE FLORENCE'S THIRD ARTICLE	87
VII	AT SIKASSO	106
VIII	MORILIRÉ	114
IX	BY SUPERIOR ORDERS	130
X	THE NEW ESCORT	144
XI	WHAT'S TO BE DONE?	160
XII	THE FOREST GRAVE	172

INTRODUCTION

Though Jules Verne is perhaps best known as a founder and master of science fiction, this art-form did not by any means exhaust his literary genius. The wide scope of his interests, and the variety of his style, are well shown in his posthumous work, *L'Étonnante Aventure de la Mission Barsac.*

Its opening sentence recalls Conan Doyle: as Kenneth Allott points out in his biography of Verne, "It is the very accent of Watson about to relate another of the cases of Sherlock Holmes." The rest of the chapter almost outdoes Edgar Wallace. Chapter III might have been written by one of the romantic novelists of the nineteenth century. The rest of Book I, with its adventures in the African bush and the forebodings of its witch-doctor, is reminiscent of Rider Haggard. Only in Book II does Jules Verne, master of science fiction, come into his own.

The whole narrative presents another remarkable contrast and raises an interesting question. There is a light-heartedness about much of Book I and some of the early chapters of Book II which recalls not the aged valetudinarian of Amiens, crippled, bereaved and seriously ill, but the brilliant young author and keen amateur yachtsman whose work had taken Paris by storm and who saw endless literary vistas opening before him. Yet there is the clearest internal evidence that most of Book II and some sections of Book I were written very late in their author's life—and, indeed, that publication may have been deliberately withheld until after his death.

The explanation may be that this was a project which Verne long had in mind. He may have begun work on this narrative and written much of it fairly early in his career, and then revised and re-revised it time and again as his mood and outlook altered, and finally have decided to make it his swan-song, the very last of his works, to appear posthumously as his epitaph. One strange result of this decision was that in Britain, where he has so very many admirers, the book has—so far as I can ascertain—never yet been published!

It may, indeed, seem strange that so extraordinary a work should have gone so long untranslated. Here, however, the explanation may be simple : in commercial terms, the market had been glutted. Verne's writings varied greatly in quality, especially in his later years when he systematically "over wrote" himself. At last, I imagine, his work had lost much of its appeal; moreover, it was rivalled by a new generation of science fiction writers, foremost of whom was H. G. Wells. This may explain why not only *The Barsac Mission* but a number of Verne's later works, remarkable though they are, have not so far found publication in Britain.

Even in the early part of Book I, the hands of the ageing Verne can be traced. The sardonic account of French politics in Chapter II may be based on his experience of the municipal government of Amiens. The absurd M. Poncin may be derived from the dislike which both the literary artist and the scientific worker feel for the mere juggler with meaningless figures. On the other hand, Verne's ideal of the French officer, austerely devoted to duty and yet cultured and humane, is enshrined in the character of Captain Marcenay.

What the Central Bank Affair described in Chapter I has to do with the rest of the narrative; what the mysterious power is that hovers so menacingly over the activities of the Barsac Mission, will appear later. For an answer to such questions, as well as for an explanation of the strange phenomena which the Mission encounters, the inexplicable roaring in the air and the inexplicable grooves in the soil, the reader must consult Book II of Verne's masterpiece, separately published in this series under the title *The City in the Sahara*.

A few alterations may have been made to adapt this work for an English-speaking public; for example, measures have been shown in British, instead of Metric, units. The names of a few of the characters have had to be altered, as they might have given rise to misunderstanding or annoyance by clashing with those of actual people. I have also taken the liberty, found necessary by most of Verne's other translators, of abbreviating or omitting a few passages of minor interest.

I. O. E.

CHAPTER I

THE CENTRAL BANK BUSINESS

CERTAINLY the audacious robbery which the press featured as "The Central Bank Business," and which was front-page news for a whole fortnight, has not yet been forgotten. Few crimes aroused so much attention, for few combined so much mystery with so much audacity, gained so much booty, or were performed with so ferocious an energy. Though it occurred at the beginning of the century, a description of the episode can still be read with interest.

The robbery took place at the DK Branch of the Central Bank, situated near the Stock Exchange, at the corner of Threadneedle Street; its Manager was Lewis Robert Blazon, son of Lord Blazon.

The Branch occupies a large room divided by a long oak counter. It is entered at the street corner by a glass-panelled door, reached from a vestibule at pavement level. Inside, on the left, behind a strong iron grille, is a strong-room from which a door, also furnished with a grille, leads into the main office, where the clerks work. On the right, the oak counter is broken by the usual flap, affording access between the part open to the public and that reserved for the clerks. At the back of this opens the Manager's office with an inner room having no other entrance; then a corridor flanks the wall along Threadneedle Street, giving access to a hall used by all the building's occupants.

On the one side this hall leads out past the messengers' box to Threadneedle Street. On the other, beyond the foot of the main stair, it is entered by a double glass-panelled door which conceals the entrance to the cellars and the service stair facing it.

At the moment when the incident began, at twenty to five exactly, the five employees of the Branch were occupied with their work. Two were busy writing. The three others were attending to clients leaning on the counter. The cashier was counting up the receipts, which, this being settlement day, amounted to the impressive total of £72,079 2s. 4d.

In twenty minutes the bank would be closed and the steel shutters pulled down; then, a little later, the staff would disperse for the day. The heavy rumbling of the traffic and the noise of the crowd could be faintly heard through the door, whose glass was obscured by the gathering dusk of this November evening.

It was at that moment that the door opened and a man entered. After a rapid glance he turned and made a gesture with his right hand, holding up the thumb and two fingers to indicate the number three. Even had their attention been aroused, the clerks would not have been able to see this gesture, hidden as it was behind the half-opened door; and even if they had seen it they would never have dreamed of associating it with the number of clients at the counter.

This signal—if it was one—having been given, the man reopened the door, let it swing-to behind him, and took his place behind one of the clients, waiting to be attended to in his turn.

A clerk got up, came towards him and asked :

"Can I help you, sir?"

"Thanks, I'll wait," answered the new-comer, indicating by a movement of his hand that he wanted to deal with the clerk nearest to him.

Having satisfied his conscience, the other clerk went back to his work, and the man went on waiting, nobody paying any more attention to him.

His strange appearance would however have justified careful study. He was a tall determined-looking man, his build suggesting unusual strength. A splendid light-coloured beard fringed his sunburnt face. It would be impossible to judge his social status from his clothing, for a long silk dust-coat covered him down to the feet.

The client having finished his business, the man in the dust-coat took his place and explained his wishes to the clerk.

THE CENTRAL BANK BUSINESS 13

Hardly had the client gone out when the door opened to admit a second personage as strange as the first, of whom indeed he seemed to be a sort of replica. Similar in height and in build, and with a similar beard fringing his bronzed face, he also wore a dust-coat long enough to hide his clothing.

This new-comer behaved like his counterpart. He waited patiently behind one of the two clients leaning on the counter; then, when his turn came, he engaged the clerk in conversation while the client went out.

As before, the door opened at once. A third individual entered and took his place behind the last of the three clients. Of medium height, short and square-built, his swarthy face partly obscured by a black beard and his clothing concealed by a long grey overcoat, he offered both differences from and resemblances to his predecessors.

Finally, when the last of the three clients had finished his business and given up his place, it was two men whom the door admitted. These men, one of whom seemed gifted with herculean strength, were dressed in the long overcoats commonly known as ulsters, which the rigour of the season did not yet justify; and their bronzed faces, like those of the three others, were abundantly garnished with beards.

Their method of entering was strange; the taller came in first; then, when hardly inside, he stopped so as to hide his companion who, pretending to have got caught in the doorhandle, was subjecting this to some mysterious operation. The pause lasted only an instant, and the door swung shut. But by that time, though it still had its inside handle, so that it could let people out, its outside handle had vanished, so that none could enter from the street. As for knocking to get admittance, nobody would have thought of this, for a notice, placed surreptitiously on the door, announced to the public that the Branch had shut down for the day.

The clerks never suspected that they were now cut off from the outer world, and if they had known it this would only have made them smile. Why should they be uneasy, right in the heart of the City, at the busiest moment of the day, when they could hear the din of the activity in the street, from which only a thin sheet of glass separated them?

The other two clerks politely came to meet these entrants, for they knew that the clocks were on the verge of striking five: it would be in order to get rid of these tiresome intruders in a few minutes. One of these late-comers accepted their attention; while the other, the bigger of the two, refused them and asked for a word with the Manager.

"I'll see if he's there," he was told.

The clerk went through the inner door and returned at once.

"If you would be good enough to step this way?" he suggested, opening the counter-flap.

The man in the ulster entered the inner office while the clerk, having closed the door behind him, went back to his work.

What took place between the Branch Manager and his visitor? The staff afterwards stated that they knew nothing. The enquiry which ensued could only surmise, and even to-day nobody knows what happened behind that door.

One thing at least is certain, that hardly two minutes had elapsed since the door closed when it opened again and the man in the ulster re-appeared on the threshold.

In an impersonal tone, and without addressing himelf to anyone in particular: "Please," he said calmly, "the Manager would like a word with the cashier."

"Very well, Sir," answered the clerk. Turning round, he exclaimed: "Store!"

"Yes, Mr. Barclay?"

"The Chief's asking for you."

"I'll be there," replied the cashier.

With the punctiliousness inherent in men of his profession, he threw into the gaping strong-room a brief-case and three packages duly labelled and containing the day's takings. The heavy door swung-to with a dull thud; then, having closed his window, he came out of his barred room, which he carefully shut behind him, and went towards the Manager's office. The stranger, who was waiting in front of it, stepped aside and then followed him in.

When he entered the office, Store was surprised to realize that the man who was supposed to have called him was not there, and that the room was empty. But time was not allowed him to investigate the mystery. Attacked from behind, his throat seized in an iron grip, it was in vain that he tried to struggle, to call for help. . . . The murderous hands increased their grasp until, his breath failing, he dropped unconscious to the floor.

This ferocious attack took place silently. In the outer office the clerks were quietly working, four of them facing the clients across the counter, the fifth absorbed in his calculations.

The man in the ulster paused to wipe a drop of sweat from his forehead, then stooped over his victim. In a trice the cashier was gagged and bound.

This task completed, he pulled the door ajar and glanced into the main office. Satisfied, he coughed quietly, as though to attract the attention of the four clients; then, his end attained, he flung open the door which concealed him.

This was the signal—no doubt pre-arranged—for a fantastic scene. While the man in the ulster crossed the room in a single bound, fell like a thunderbolt on the lonely arithmetician and throttled him pitilessly, the victim's four colleagues underwent a similar fate.

The client at the far end of the counter thrust up the flap and leapt through the opening; taking from behind the clerk who had been facing him, he threw him to the ground. Of the three others, two reached over, looped their hands around the necks of the clerks in front of them, and banged their heads on the oak counter-top. The fourth, the smallest of stature, not being able to grasp his adversary from across the distance between them, leaped right over the counter, and seized him by the neck, the violence of his attack increased ten-fold by its speed.

Not a single cry was uttered, and the drama had lasted only thirty seconds.

When their victims lost consciousness, the garrotters finished putting them out of action. The scheme had been studied in detail and nothing had gone amiss. They did not hesitate. Together taking the risk of asphyxiating their victims, they stuffed their mouths full of cotton-wool and gagged them. Then they pulled their hands behind their backs and pinioned them, tied their feet firmly together, and trussed up their bodies in a skein of fine steel wire.

The work was completed at once; then the assailants stood up simultaneously.

"The shutter!" The order came from the man who had asked to see the Manager, and who seemed to command the others.

Three of the bandits hastened to turn the cranks of the metal shutter. The iron sheets began to descend over the entrance, gradually muffling the noise from outside.

This operation was half completed when suddenly the telephone-bell rang.

"Stop!" exclaimed the chief of the robbers.

The shutter having been halted in its downward movement, he went across to the apparatus and picked up the receiver. The following conversation began, the four garrotters, now standing motionless, hearing only the half of it.

"Hallo!"

"I'm listening."

"That you, Blazon?"

"Yes."

"That's queer. I don't recognize your voice."

"It's a faulty line."

"Not at our end."

"Well, it is here. I don't recognize your voice either."

"I'm Mr. Leonard."

"Oh, yes! ... yes! I can recognize you now.

"Can you tell me, Blazon, whether the van has arrived yet?"

"Not yet," the bandit replied, after hesitating slightly.

"When it comes, send it back to S Branch. They've just telephoned to say that an important deposit came in after they'd closed down and sent off the cash."

"A large sum?"

"Fairly. About twenty thousand pounds."

The robber gave an exclamation of surprise.

"You'll give the message? I can rely on you?"

"You can rely on me."

"Good night, Blazon."

"Good night."

The stranger replaced the receiver; for a moment he remained motionless, thinking.

He suddenly made up his mind. Calling his accomplices round him, "We'll have to hurry, boys," he told them in a low voice, beginning to undress hastily. "Hurry up! Somebody give me that fellow's hide."

He pointed to Store, still completely unconscious.

In a twinkling of the eye the man was stripped of his clothing, and his aggressor donned them, although the garments were a little on the small side. Having found the keys of the counting-house in one of the pockets, he opened first the cashier's office and then the strong-room, from which he took the numbered packages, the brief-case, and the bundles of securities.

Hardly had he finished when a vehicle could be heard stopping at the edge of the pavement. Almost at once a knock was heard on the glass-panelled door half covered by the metallic curtain.

"Look out!" the chief of the garrotters said quickly, eking out his words with gestures. "Off with your coats, let them see your clothing, get into your places and be ready! Take care you don't miss whoever comes in!... And no noise, mind!... Then shut the door and don't open it except to me!"

While speaking, and taking with him the brief-case and several bundles of the securities, he went over to the door. He signed to three of his accomplices to take the places of the clerks, whom they thrust beneath the counter, while the fourth waited beside the door. He opened this sharply and at once the noise from the street seemed to get louder.

A delivery van had indeed pulled up before the entrance; its lights could be seen gleaming in the darkness. The driver, perched on his seat, was chatting with a man who was standing on the edge of the pavement. It was that man, a cashier at the Central Bank, who had knocked at the door a few minutes earlier.

Without hurrying, and dodging the passers-by who flowed on like a torrent, the audacious bandit crossed the pavement and went up to the vehicle.

"Good evening," he said.

"Evening!" the two men replied.

The driver, after looking at the new-comer, seemed taken aback.

"Hullo! ... It isn't Store!" he exclaimed.

"It's his day off, and I'm acting for him."

Then, speaking to the man standing on the pavement, he said:

"Well, old man, what about giving me a hand?"

"What with?"

"One of our bags. There's a lot of money come in to-day, and it's heavy."

"Yes, but," replied the cashier, hesitating, "I'm not allowed to leave the vehicle."

"Nonsense! It's only a minute! And, anyhow, I'll take your place. One of the clerks will give you a hand while I'm putting in the brief-case and the securities."

The cashier went off without further protest and entered the door, which shut behind him.

"Now, my friend," the man who had taken the place of Store said to the driver: "Open her up."

"Right!" the driver agreed.

The body of the van had no exit at the back or at its sides, its only opening being a double door consisting of two metal sheets, placed behind the coachman's box. Thus the risks of a robbery were reduced to a minimum.

To gain access to the vehicle, the seat, half of which was movable, had to be swung up. But, as he only needed to put a few packets in one of the pigeon-holes along the sides, the driver did not think it worth while taking so much trouble, and simply pushed back the flaps.

"Let's have the brief-case," he said.

Having received it, the driver, bending forward across his seat, vanished as far as the waist in the vehicle's interior, his legs acting as a counterpoise.

Thus placed, he could not see his self-appointed colleague climbing on to the step and on to the seat, so as to come between him and the reins. Leaning over the driver, the sham cashier, as though curious to see what was inside the van, thrust the upper part of his body into it; and suddenly his arm gave a violent thrust into the darkness.

If any of the numerous passers-by had thought of looking at that moment, they would have seen the coachman's legs suddenly become strangely rigid, then fall inert on the floor of his seat while his torso sagged down on its far side.

The man quickly seized this inert body by the belt, and thrust it into the midst of the bags and packets within the vehicle.

This series of actions, carried out with precision and with marvellous audacity, took only a few moments. The passers-by continued peacefully on their way, without the slightest suspicion of these unusual happenings taking place so near them in the crowd.

The man again leaned forward into the vehicle, so as not to be dazzled by the street-lamps, and stared into its interior. On its floor, in the midst of a pool of blood which spread even as he watched it, lay the driver, a knife thrust into the base of his skull. He was no longer moving; he had been struck down as though by lightning.

The murderer, fearing that the blood would end by overflowing on to the road, stepped over the bench and went bodily into the vehicle; taking off the driver's coat, he used it to staunch that terrible wound. Then, having pulled out the knife and carefully wiped its blade, and his own red-stained hands, he shut the doors, sure that the blood, if it kept on flowing, would soak into fabric as though into a sponge.

Having taken this precaution, he got down from the vehicle, crossed the pavement and rapped in the agreed manner at the door of the Bank; it was opened at once, then it closed behind him.

"That fellow?" he asked, on entering.

Someone pointed to the counter.

"With the others, trussed up."

"Good! Off with his clothing! Quick!"

While the others hastened to obey, he took off Store's uniform and replaced it by that of the other cashier.

"Two of you will stay here," he commanded, while this transformation was being accomplished. "The others can come with me to get the swag."

Without waiting for any reply he re-opened the door, went out with his two acolytes following him, got back on to the driving-seat and clambered into the interior of the vehicle to start pillaging it.

One after the other, he gave the packages to his accomplices, who took them into the Agency. Its door, fastened wide open, threw a square of light on to the pavement. The passers-by, coming out of the darkness of the street and then going back into it, crossed without even noticing that strip of brightness. Nothing could have kept them from going in. But that notion did not occur to anyone, and the crowd flowed on, regardless of a transaction which was no concern of theirs and of which they had no reason to be suspicious.

In a few minutes the vehicle had been emptied. The door closed, the booty was sorted out. The documents went on one side, the specie on the other. The first, ruthlessly rejected, were scattered about the floor. The bank notes were divided into five portions, one taken by each of the men, who padded out his chest with them.

"And the bags?" asked one of the bandits.

"Stuff them into your pockets," the chief replied. "I'll look after what's left in the van."

He was at once obeyed.

"Just a minute," he exclaimed. "First let's get things settled. When I've gone, you'll come back here and finish lowering the shutter. Then," he continued, "you go out along the corridor. The last man will lock and double-lock the door and chuck the key down the drain. The main hall's at the far end and you know the way out."

With one finger he pointed to the Manager's office.

"Don't forget that fellow. You know what we agreed?"

"Yes, yes," they replied. "Leave that to us."

Just as he was going off, he stopped again.

"Hell!" he said. "I'd forgotten about the chief. He ought to have a list of the other Branches."

One of them showed him a yellow notice, stuck on the inside of the glass. He scanned it rapidly.

"As for the coats," he said, after he had found the address of S Branch, "throw them in a corner. It doesn't matter if they're found. The one thing is that they shouldn't be seen on our backs. You know where we meet. Now let's get on with it."

The rest of the bags of gold and silver were carried out into the vehicle.

"That all?" enquired one of the "porters."

"Curse it, no! What about my togs?"

The other dashed off, to return almost at once with the clothes which had first been replaced by those of the cashier Store, and slung them inside the vehicle.

"Is that everything this time?" he asked again.

"Yes. And don't hang about!" was the answer.

The man disappeared into the bank. The iron shutter closed right down.

Then the improvised driver grasped the reins and aroused the horses with a cut of the whip. The vehicle went off, not stopping until it reached S Branch.

The false driver entered boldly and went up to the counting-house.

"I think you've got a letter for me?"

The cashier looked up to see who was speaking.

"Well!" he exclaimed, "It isn't Baudruc."

"No, it isn't!" replied the applicant with a coarse laugh.

"I can't make the Management out," the cashier grumbled with annoyance, "sending people along whom we've never heard of."

"It's because I don't usually do this round. I was at B Branch when I was told to call here; it was a telephone call from the central office. You seem to have had a big deposit after closing time."

He made up this plausible reply on the spot.

"Yes," the cashier agreed, his suspicions notwithstanding. "All the same, it's worrying that I can't recognize you."

"What's that got to do with you?" replied the other, taken by surprise.

"There's so many thieves about. Still, all the same, we can easily settle it. I suppose you've got your credentials?"

If anything would be likely to disquiet the bandit, it was certainly such a question. How could he have his "credentials?" He didn't even know what they were. This did not, however, disquiet him. Anyone who embarks on such adventures must have certain qualities, notably an absolute sang-froid. This was something which the false cashier of the Central Bank possessed in abundance. So, if he were perturbed at hearing such a question shot at him out of the blue, he did not show it. He simply replied in the most natural voice, "Of course! That goes without saying."

A simple process of reasoning convinced him that these "credentials," which admittedly he ought to have on him, must consist of some material object which the employees of the

Central Bank would always carry. By rummaging through the clothing he had taken, he could certainly come across them.

"I'll show you," he added calmly, sitting down on a bench and turning out his pockets.

He took out an assortment of documents, letters, notes of instruction and others, all badly folded and rubbed. Imitating the clumsiness of workmen when their broad fingers, more adept at coarser tasks, have to deal with paper-work, he unfolded them one after the other.

Soon he found a printed document, its blank spaces filled in by hand, stating that the man named Baudruc was authorized to act as chief cashier at the Central Bank. This was plainly the one he was looking for, and yet the difficulty still remained. The name on the document might form the greatest of his dangers, for the cashier knew Baudruc and was surprised at not having to deal with him.

Without losing any of his coolness, the audacious bandit at once thought of the necessary trick. While the cashier's attention was turned elsewhere, he tore the document in two; he let the upper half, which bore the name, get mixed with the other papers and held out the lower half.

"No luck," he exclaimed as though annoyed, "I've got half of my credentials, but not the rest."

"Half of them?" repeated the cashier.

"Yes. They're old and they've got badly worn, always being in my pocket. They've come in two, and I've carelessly left half at home."

The cashier grunted uneasily.

"Oh well, that's enough," said the robber, getting up and moving towards the door. "I've been told to come and pick up your spondulics, well I've come. You'd rather not let me have them? Then keep them. You can settle it with the Head Office. It's none of my business."

The indifference he showed was more effective than the best arguments and still more was the menacing phrase which he had fired, like a Parthian shot, as he went off. "No trouble!" that is the eternal watchword of every employee on earth.

"Wait a minute!" exclaimed the cashier, calling him back. "Let me see your credentials."

"Here they are!" replied the applicant.

"There's the Chief's signature," the cashier agreed with satisfaction. Then, at last making up his mind, "Here's the money," he said, handing over a sealed packet. "If you'd just sign the receipt?"

The applicant, having put down some name or other, went off, still looking annoyed.

"Good night!" he said brusquely, as though irritated by the suspicion levelled against him.

Once outside, he hurried to the vehicle, climbed on the seat and vanished into the night.

Thus was the robbery completed which aroused so much excitement.

As is well known, it was discovered that very evening, more quickly indeed than the culprits had expected. The branch locked up, the staff rendered helpless, the driver of the van put out of the way, they could reasonably have thought that nothing would be noticed until next morning. Then the caretaker, going to give the daily sweeping-up, would be certain to give the alarm, but until then there was every chance that the incident would remain a secret.

In actual fact, things turned out quite differently.

At half past seven the van was discovered, in a lonely street behind Hyde Park, by one of the Central Office staff who was on his way home. The employee, surprised to see a vehicle belonging to the Bank standing in this obscure and deserted street, had pushed open the door, which was unfastened; and, lighting a match, he had found the driver's body, already cold. He had at once given the alarm.

Then the telephone got busy in every direction. Before eight, a squad of police surrounded the empty van while a crowd gathered before the DK Branch, where another squad was having the doors forced open by a locksmith.

The enquiry began at once. By good fortune none of the employees was dead, though to tell the truth they were not far from it. Three parts stifled by the gags, their mouths stuffed full of rags and cotton wool, they were lying unconscious when help arrived, and no doubt they would have passed away before morning.

When, after an hour's treatment, they regained consciousness, the information which they could give was very vague. Five bearded men, some covered by long dust-coats, the others by ulsters, had assaulted and overcome them. They knew nothing else.

There was no reason to doubt their sincerity. Right at the start of the enquiry, indeed, the five coats had been found, as if the malefactors had wanted to leave signs of their presence. But these garments, carefully examined by the keenest sleuths of Scotland Yard, disclosed nothing regarding those who had left them. Made of commonplace material, they bore no indication of tailor or dealer, and no doubt this was why they had been left.

All this did not say very much, and yet the police inspector had to give up hopes of learning anything else. He vainly examined the witnesses from every point of view. Their stories did not vary, and he could get nothing further out of them.

The last witness was the caretaker. The offices which he had to look after were too numerous for him to supervise them properly, and that day he had noticed nothing unusual. If the thieves had passed him, as was quite likely, he would have taken them for members of the staff.

Urged to ransack his memory, he mentioned four men employed in the building who had passed him about the time of the robbery, or a little later. Enquiry showed that all four were above suspicion; they had simply been going home.

The caretaker also mentioned a coalman who had called about half past seven, a little before the police arrived; the fellow was carrying a large sack, and the caretaker had noticed him simply because it was so unusual to deliver coal at such an hour. The coalman had enquired after an office on the fifth floor and had been so insistent that the caretaker had admitted him and shown him the service stairs.

The coalman had gone up, only to descend a quarter of an hour later, still carrying his sack: he explained that he had mistaken the address. Panting, like someone who had just climbed with a heavy burden up several flights of stairs, he had gone out into the street; then, having deposited his sack in a barrow standing beside the pavement, he had gone slowly away.

"Do you know," the inspector enquired, "what firm the coalman belonged to?"

The caretaker replied that he didn't.

The fifth floor tenant had confirmed that a man, saying he had some coal to deliver, had rung at the service door about half past seven. When the servant who answered the bell had told him he must be mistaken, he had simply gone away. The only clash between the two statements was that the servant maintained that, whatever the caretaker might say, the man was not carrying a sack.

"He might have left it below while he went up," the inspector surmised.

None the less, that supposition seemed inadequate when there were found, in the passage leading to the cellars, the contents of a bag of anthracite, which the caretaker said had not been there a few hours earlier. The evidence indicated that the mysterious coalman must have emptied the sack he was carying in that corner. Then what was he carrying? Because— the caretaker was quite certain on this point—the sack seemed to be no less full, and no lighter, when he went out than when he arrived.

"Never mind about that for the moment," the inspector decided, giving up trying to solve an insoluble problem. "That can be cleared up later."

THE CENTRAL BANK BUSINESS 27

For the time being he had to follow a trail which he thought more important, and he was not going to swerve from it.

Not all the personnel of the Branch had been found. The most important of all, the Manager, did not answer the roll-call. Mr. Lewis Robert Blazon had vanished.

The employees could give no information about this. All they knew was that, shortly before five, a client, who had gone to see the Manager, had called in the cashier Store, who had answered the summons and had not reappeared. A few minutes later came the attack. As for Mr. Blazon, nobody had seen him since.

The conclusion was obvious. While it was beyond doubt that the Branch had been taken by assault by five brigands from outside, it was no less clear that they had an accomplice in the office and that this accomplice could be no other than its Manager.

That was why, without waiting for the results of a more detailed enquiry, a warrant was at once made out against Lewis Robert Blazon, Manager of the DK Branch of the Central Bank, suspected of complicity in robbery and conspiracy to murder. That was why his description, which, unlike that of his accomplices, was well-known, was telegraphed in all directions.

As the culprit had not yet had time to leave England, he could surely be apprehended either in some inland town or seaport, an achievement on which the police soon hoped to pride themselves.

With this agreeable prospect, inspector and detectives went back to their respective beds.

Then, that very night, at two in the morning, five men, some cleanshaven and others with their bronzed faces partly concealed by a moustache, travelled to Southampton by the London train. After having collected from the guard's van several parcels and a large and heavy trunk, they went by cab to the docks; at the quay waited a steamer of about two thousand tons, whose funnel was vomiting smoke.

On the four o'clock tide, when everybody at Southampton was asleep, the steamer cast off and made for the open sea.

No attempt was made to interfere with her. And why, anyhow, should that honest vessel be suspected, openly loaded as it was with freight, miscellaneous but legitimate, consigned to Kotonou, the seaport of Dahomey?

The steamer, therefore, went off quite peaceably, with her freight, her five passengers, their packages and their large trunk. One of them, the strongest, had had it stowed in his cabin when the police, breaking off their enquiry, were seeking a well-earned rest.

As is well known, the enquiry, which was resumed the following day and continued for some time, never reached a definite conclusion: the five malefactors remained unidentified, and Lewis Robert Blazon could not be traced. No gleam of light shone on the impenetrable mystery. No one so much as traced the firm that employed the coalman who for a moment had attracted the attention of the police. The business had to be classed among the unsolved mysteries.

The solution of the riddle is given for the first time, and once and for all, in the following narrative. It is for the reader to say whether he could imagine anything more unexpected and more strange.

CHAPTER II

A JOURNEY OF INVESTIGATION

At the time Konakry, though the capital of French Guinea and the Residency of the Governor-General, was little more than a hamlet.

On the 27th November that hamlet was holding a fête. Responding to the Governor's pressing invitation, the whole population was going seawards to give a warm welcome to some important travellers who had just disembarked.

Certainly they were important enough. Seven in all, they formed the higher staff of the Extra-Parliamentary Commission instructed by the Central Administration of France to carry out a journey of investigation into the part of the French Soudan known as the Niger Bend. To tell the truth, it was not quite of their own volition that the President of the Council and the Minister for the Colonies had sent out that Mission and ordered that investigation. They had so to speak been compelled to do so by the insistence of the Chambre des Deputés and by the need to close an oratorical tournament which did nothing but hold up business.

Several months previously, as the outcome of a debate on that part of Africa which the Mission was ordered to explore, the Chamber had been split into two equal halves, led into the combat by two irreconcilable leaders. One was called Barsac, the other Baudrières.

The first was plump, not to say tubby, wearing a luxurious black beard like a fan. He was a Meridional from Provence, fond of resounding words and gifted if not with eloquence at any rate with a certain fluency, but a cheerful and sympathetic fellow at heart.

The second represented one of the Departments of the North, and—if so bold an expression be allowed—he represented it also in appearance. Lean in face and body, a scanty drooping moustache ornamenting his thin lips, awkward and dogmatic, he was one of nature's pessimists. While his colleague seemed to expand generously, he seemed to be folded in upon himself, locking up his soul like a miser's strong-box.

Deputies of long standing, they both specialized in colonial problems, and were regarded as authorities upon such matters. Yet it seemed marvellous how their patient studies led them to such opposite conclusions. For the fact is that they very seldom agreed. Whatever point it was that Barsac raised, you could bet ten to one that Baudrières would demand to be heard simply in order to say just the opposite. As their speeches cancelled out, the Chamber was usually driven to the recourse of voting in the sense indicated by the Minister.

But this time neither Barsac nor Baudrières had been willing to yield an inch and the dispute threatened to go on for ever. It had begun on the subject of a law proposed by the former, to create five deputies' seats in Senegal, Gambia, Upper Guinea, and the part of the French Soudan situated west of the Niger, and to extend the vote, granted their eligibility, to the coloured peoples without distinction of race. At once, following his usual practice, Baudrières has risen energetically to oppose Barsac's suggestion, and the two adversaries had bombarded each other's heads with a barrage of arguments.

The one, citing the authority of many civil and military travellers familiar with the region, declared that the negroes had risen to a high degree of civilization. He added that it availed little to have suppressed slavery unless the subject peoples were given the same rights as their masters, and, in a series of perorations which the Chambre applauded vociferously, he pronounced the mighty words *"liberté, egalité, et fraternité."*

His adversary affirmed, on the other hand, that the negroes still wallowed in the most shameful savagery, and that there could be no more a question of consulting them than anyone consults a sick child about his medicine. He added that this was not the time to attempt so dangerous an experiment, and that it would be better to reinforce the army of occupation in those countries, as there were disquieting signs that trouble was brewing. He invoked as many civil and military opinions as his opponent, forecast further armed interventions in the region, and declared with a burst of patriotic energy that lands won by French blood were forever sacred and inviolable. He too was applauded frantically.

The Colonial Minister was hard put to it to decide between them. He saw truth in both standpoints. While the coloured races living in and near the Niger Bend were getting accustomed to French rule, while education was making headway among peoples hitherto plunged in ignorance, and while security was rapidly advancing, it was equally true that at the moment the situation was changing unfavourably. News was coming in of disturbances and raids; whole villages had, for reasons unknown, been abandoned by their inhabitants. There were even vague rumours, which could not be ignored, that some independent power was being set up at some point unknown on African soil.

Each of the two orators found the Minister's arguments so favourable to himself that they crowed over one another, and the discussion proceeded until one of the excited Deputies shouted in the midst of the uproar :

"As they can't agree, they'd better go and find out !"

The Minister replied that the region had been so often explored that there was no need to discover it anew, but none the less he was prepared to take the opinion of the Chamber. If they thought a journey of investigation would be worth while, he would gladly associate himself with it and would place the Expedition under the leadership of whichever of its members they cared to nominate.

This proposal was quite successful. The session was closed, and the Minister was invited to constitute a Mission to traverse the region included in the Niger Bend and to prepare a report on which the Chamber might come to a decision.

It was not so easy to agree when it came to nominating the Deputy who was to lead the Mission, and on a double count the number of votes for Barsac and Baudrières were exactly equal.

However, the matter had to be settled.

"*Parbleu!* Let's nominate both of them!" exclaimed one of those humourists never lacking in an assembly of Frenchmen.

This idea was welcomed enthusiastically by the Chamber, whose members no doubt saw that it was one way of not hearing any more talk about the Colonies for several months. Barsac and Baudrières were accordingly elected, the question of supreme authority being settled by their respective ages. These having been ascertained, the privilege fell to Barsac, who was the elder by three days, and Baudrières had to resign himself, to his extreme disgust, to being nothing but a subordinate.

To this nucleus of a Mission the Government had added several other personalities, less colourful indeed but perhaps better qualified.

Among these was Dr. Châtonnay, a well-known doctor, he was quite competent, and his cheerful face, more than five feet eight inches from the ground, was surmounted with curly hair as white as snow—though he was hardly fifty years old—and crossed by a bristly moustache of the same colour. He was a fine man, that Doctor Châtonnay, intelligent and light-hearted, continually laughing with a noise like escaping steam.

Equally noticeable was M. Isidore Tassin, correspondent of the Geographical Society, a little dry peremptory man, passionately and exclusively devoted to his subject. As for the other members of the Mission, Mm. Poncin, Quirieu, and Heyrieux, employed by various Ministries, hardly anyone would have noticed them. Without pronounced individuality, they were just as much people as anybody else.

Around this official core, an eighth traveller moved very officiously. He was called Amédée Florence, and his task was to keep in touch to the best of his ability with the great daily paper, *L'Éxpansion Française,* of which he was an active and lucid reporter.

The arrival of these personages was bound to evoke oratory. Anyone who takes part in administration or government is not going to be content, when he meets anybody, with a shake of the hand and a "Good morning!"; he considers it essential to say something for the benefit of history. Meanwhile his audience, invariably amused, often though they have encountered it before, by the absurdity of such a formality, form a circle around the orators.

Complying with protocol, the Governor, M. Valdonne, accompanied by his chief officials whom he took care to introduce, solemnly bade welcome to these important visitors when they arrived, if not from Heaven at any rate from beyond the ocean. Nevertheless, to do him justice, he was brief and his short harangue won the success it deserved.

Barsac, in replying as chief of the mission, uttered the following words:

"Monsieur le Governeur, Messieurs," he began, in accents of gratitude—and of the Midi!—after having coughed to clear his throat, "my colleagues and I are profoundly moved by the words we have just heard. We regard the cordiality of your welcome as a favourable augury, at the moment when we are about to begin an enterprise whose difficulties cannot be exaggerated. We know that, under the generous administration of their government, these regions, formerly explored in the midst of so many perils by the hardy pioneers of *la patrie*, at last know the Peace of France, if I may use this somewhat pompous expression borrowed from our Roman ancestors.

"That is why, here, on the threshold of this magnificent town of Konakry, surrounded by the serried ranks of our compatriots, we feel as if we had never left France. That is why, when making our way into the interior, we shall not be leaving it even then, for the toiling multitudes of these countries have already become the citizens of an enlarged and extended France. May our presence in their midst give them the proof of the watchful care of the public administration!

May it still more increase, if this be possible, their attachment to *la patrie*, their devotion to the Republic!"

M. le Governeur Valdonne then gave the usual signal for "spontaneous" applause, while Barsac stepped backwards and Baudrières came to the front.

As a result of endless consultations in the Minister's office, it had been decided that Baudrières should be not the assistant leader but the *associate* leader of the expedition. Mysterious power of words!—the result seemed to be that if Barsac took the lead at an official ceremony, Baudrières came immediately after him. Thus was solved the ticklish question of precedence.

"Monsieur le Governeur, Messieurs," Baudrières commenced, thus cutting short the applause evoked by the peroration of his predecessor, "I associate myself completely with the eloquent words of my eminent colleague and friend. As he has explained, each of us must state exactly the difficulties and dangers which our expedition may meet. For the difficulties, we shall do our best to overcome them ourselves. As to the dangers, they will not dismay us, because between them and ourselves are interposed the bayonets of France.

"You must therefore allow me to give, as we first set foot on African soil, a heartfelt salute to the escort which will keep at bay the possibility of danger. Gentlemen, in saluting that small escort, it is to the Army—for is not the Army there in the person of the humblest trooper we meet?—it is to the Army, I say, that I address my greeting. It is the Army, then, so dear to every French heart, which participates in our work, and it is through them that this obscure undertaking will increase, as has so often been done by the glorious adventures to which they are accustomed, the prestige of our country and the glory of our Republic!"

Again there came a burst of applause, as much stimulated and as much spontaneous as the other; then the assembly moved on to the Residency, where the leading members of the Mission were to be accommodated for the three days devoted to settling the final details of their programme.

A JOURNEY OF INVESTIGATION

That programme was vast. The region involved in the Barsac's proposed law exceeded 1,000,000 square miles. If there could be no question of visiting the whole of this immense expanse, about three times the size of France, at least a route had been worked out complicated enough to give the impression that its results had some chance of conforming to the truth. Indeed, that route would cover more than 1,500 miles for some members of the Mission and nearly 2,500 for the others.

The expedition would in fact have to split up during the journey so as to extend as far as possible the course of the enquiry. On leaving Konakry, the Mission would first proceed to Kankan. Thence it would continue as far as Sikasso, the largest town in the Kenedougou.

It would be here, about seven hundred and fifty miles from the sea, that the expedition would divide. One half, under the leadership of Baudrières, would return southwards and at last reach the Ivory Coast. The other section would continue eastwards under Barsac and reach the Niger at Saye; then, marching parallel to the river, it would attain its objective on the Dahomey coast. Because unavoidable delays and detours might prolong the journeys, it would not be until August that Baudrières would arrive at Grand-Bassam, or until October that Barsac would arrive at Kotonou.

Thus it was a question of a long journey, but M. Isidore Tassin could not flatter himself that it would allow him to establish any important geographical fact as yet unknown. To tell the truth, the presence of a corresponding member of the Geographical Society had not been accounted for, the task of discovering the Niger Bend being about as hopeful as that of discovering America. But M. Tassin was not greedy. The globe having been traversed in every direction, he knew that he would have to content himself with very little.

He was well advised in limiting his ambitions. The Niger Bend had long since ceased to be the inaccessible and mysterious region which it had once been. Indeed, the Western Sudan no longer merited the term "wild"; conquest had given place to administration—its centres were becoming more numerous, assuring more and more completely the benevolent domination of France.

Even now, when the extra-parliamentary Mission was going to traverse these regions, their pacification was not yet completed. Security was already so great, however, that there were hopes that the journey would be accomplished, if not without incident, at any rate without accident, and that it would become a walk among these peaceable peoples whom Barsac thought ripe to taste the joys of electoral politics.

The start was fixed for 1st December.

The previous night an official dinner was going to unite for the last time the members of the Mission at the Governor's table. At the end of the dinner toasts would be exchanged, as is the custom, to the obligatory accompaniment of the National Anthem, and the last wishes would be given for the success of the expedition and the glory of the Republic.

That day Barsac, tired of having wandered about in Konakry under a blazing sun, had just gone back to his room. He was fanning himself with relief, waiting for the hour at which he could take off his black coat—which whatever the temperature no official personage may dispense with during working hours—when the orderly, a man re-engaged from the colonial service who "knew all its little ways" came to tell him that two people were asking for him.

"Who are they?" asked Barsac.

"A type and his lady," was all the fellow said.

"Colonials?"

"I shouldn't think so, to judge by the look of them," the orderly replied. "The man's tall, with not much lawn on his pebble."

"His pebble?"

"He's bald! Tow-coloured whiskers and eyes like the knob of a staircase."

"You've got an imagination!" said Barsac. "And the lady?"

"The lady?"

"Yes. What's she like? Young?"

"Fairly."

"Pretty?"

"Yes—and stylish!"

Barsac absent-mindedly stroked his moustache and said, "Show them in."

While giving that order, he threw a glance, almost unconsciously, at the mirror which reflected his corpulent figure. Though he had not noticed it the clock was striking six, the exact hour—allowing for the difference of longitude—at which began the famous raid on the Central Bank.

The visitors, a man about forty years old followed by a girl of twenty to twenty-five, were shown into the room where Barsac was bracing himself for the fatigues of an official dinner by tasting the charms of indolence.

The new-comer was indeed very tall. A pair of endless legs supported a body relatively skimpy, topped by a long bony neck, the base of a long narrow head. If his eyes did not resemble the knob of a staircase, as the orderly had suggested in a most outrageous comparison, nobody could deny that they bulged, nor that his nose was large, nor that his lips were thick and hairless, a razor having pitilessly suppressed his moustache.

On the other hand whiskers, like those commonly attributed to the Austrians, and a crown of curly hair surrounding the base of a skull marvellously bare and polished, showed that the orderly was not very precise in his choice of his adjectives. "Tow-coloured," he had said. The word was not exact. Indeed, this personage was ginger.

Yet, ungainly as it was, his ugliness was appealing. His mouth suggested candour, and in his eyes there shone that sardonic goodness to which the French give the charming name of *bonhomie*.

Behind him came the young lady. Certainly the orderly, in calling her pretty, had not exaggerated. Tall, slight, with a shapely figure, her mouth red and well-shaped, her nose shapely, her eyes large and surmounted by admirably curved eyebrows, her hair abundant and as black as ink, she was really beautiful and faultlessly turned out.

When Barsac had offered chairs to his visitors, it was the man who began to speak.

"You will pardon us, Monsieur le Député, for coming to ask your help, and as there is nobody else to introduce us, you will excuse us if we do it ourselves. I'm called—you will allow me to add, for my name is absurd—I'm sorry to say I'm called Agénor de Saint-Bérain, land-owner, bachelor, and citizen of the town of Rennes."

Having thus explained his status, Agénor de Saint-Bérain made a slight pause; then, eking out his words with a gesture, he introduced:

"Miss Jane Mornas, my aunt."

"Your *aunt?*" repeated Barsac.

"Yes. Miss Mornas is really my aunt, as much as anybody can be anybody's," Agénor de Saint-Bérain assured him, while the young girl's lips parted gaily in a smile.

"M. de Saint-Bérain," she explained with a slight English accent, "insists on his status as my nephew, and never loses any opportunity of announcing our true relationship...."

"It makes me feel younger," put in her nephew.

"But," Jane Mornas continued, "once he has produced his effect and established his legal right, he agrees to reverse the position and to become once again my Uncle Agénor—that's what, within the family, he's always been since I was born."

"And it's more in accordance with my age," explained the uncle-nephew. "But let us get on. Having introduced ourselves, you will allow me, Monsieur le Député, to tell you what brings us here. Miss Mornas and I, as you see, are explorers. My aunt-niece is a fearless traveller, and I, like a good uncle-nephew, let her drag me about the world. We don't intend to stop at Konakry, but to go on into the interior, looking for new experiences. We've made all our preparations, and we were just on the point of setting off, when we heard that a Mission under your command was about to follow a route similar to our own. I pointed out to Miss Mornas that, however peaceful the country may be, I thought it best to join your Mission if you will accept us. So we have come to ask you to authorize us to make the journey with you."

"I can't see any objections in principle," replied Barsac, "but you will understand that I must consult my colleagues."

"Of course," St. Bérain agreed.

"They might be afraid that the presence of a lady would delay our progress, and would interfere with our carrying out the programme we have planned. If so. . . ."

"They needn't worry about that!" Uncle Agénor protested. "Miss Mornas is as good as a man. She would expect you to treat her not as a woman but as one of yourselves."

"Of course," Jane agreed. "I can assure you, too, that we needn't give you any trouble regarding equipment. We have got our own horses and porters. In fact we don't need anything. We've even got two Bambaras, formerly in the Senegal Tirailleurs, to be our guides and interpreters. You needn't be afraid of letting us join you."

"Well, in that case . . ." Barsac conceded. "I'll talk about it with my colleagues, and if they agree, we'll take it as settled. When shall I let you know our decision?"

"To-morrow, when you set out, because that's when we were going anyhow."

This having been agreed, the visitors took their leave.

While dining with the Governor, Barsac passed on the request to his colleagues. They received it favourably. Baudrières was the only one who had doubts about it. Not that he refused outright to have so charming a fellow-traveller, whom Barsac advocated with perhaps unnecessary warmth, but none the less he showed a certain hesitation. He thought the episode somewhat ambiguous. Was it conceivable that a young lady could set out on such a journey? No indeed, this reason could not be serious, and they had to believe that she was concealing her real purpose. This point having been raised, mightn't it be feared that her request concealed some sort of trap! Who knew, indeed, if it had some connection with the rumours which had been flying about the Ministry and the Chamber?

Grinning, the others reassured him.

"I don't know M. de Saint-Bérain nor Miss Mornas," said M. Valdonne, "but they've been in Konakry a fortnight and I've noticed them."

"You would notice one of them at least!" Barsac spoke emphatically.

"Yes, the young lady is very pretty," M. Valdonne agreed. "They came, I'm told, from St. Louis de Senegal, by the coastal steamer. Strange as it seems, they appear to be travelling simply for pleasure, just as they told M. Barsac. I can't see that it would cause the slightest inconvenience to satisfy them."

There was no further opposition, and his opinion carried the day.

This was how the Mission led by Barsac received two new recruits. It now consisted of ten members, including Amédée Florence, reporter to *L'Éxpansion Française,* but not including the porters and the escort. It was only chance which next morning favoured Pierre Marcenay, a captain in the colonial infantry and commander of the escort, in allowing him to forestall Barsac just as the latter was hurrying, as fast as a somewhat tubby man of forty could possibly hurry, to help Miss Mornay into her saddle.

"Armis cedat insigne," said Barsac, who was versed in the classics, indicating the place taken on official occasions by his badge of office.

But anyone could see that he was not greatly pleased.

CHAPTER III

LORD BLAZON OF GLENOR

WHEN this narrative began, many years had passed since Lord Blazon had gone out of his home, many years since the door of Glenor Castle—in which he dwelt near the little town of Uttoxeter in the heart of England—had been opened to admit any visitor, many years since the windows of his own rooms had been finally and firmly closed. His seclusion had been complete, absolute, since the events which had tarnished the honour of his family, smirched his name, and ruined his life.

More than sixty years before, Lord Blazon, having recently passed out of the Royal Naval Academy, had entered adult life through the front door; he had inherited from his ancestors wealth, immaculate honour, and fame.

The history of the Blazon family was indeed inseparable from that of England, for whose sake they had freely shed their blood. Before the words "my country" had gained the value which a long national existence has given them, that ideal was already deeply graven on the heart of the men of that family which, coming over with the Norman Conquest, had lived only by the sword, and by the sword wielded in their country's service. Throughout the centuries nothing had diminished the glory of their name, and never a stain had fallen on their crest.

Edward Alan Blazon was the worthy descendant of that proud line. Following his ancestor's example, he could imagine no other purpose in life but the proud cultivation of his honour, the passionate love of his country.

If atavism, heredity, whatever name be given to that strange process which makes the sons resemble their fathers, had not imparted these principles to him, his education would have inculcated them. The history of England, so full of the glories of his ancestors, must have inspired him with the wish to do as well as, if not better than, they.

At twenty-two he had married a girl belonging to one of the first families of England; and a year after their marriage a daughter was born. This was a disappointment to Edward Blazon, who waited impatiently for the birth of his second child.

He waited twenty years. It was only after that long period that Lady Blazon, whose health had been gravely impaired by her daughter's birth, gave him the son he longed for. This child was christened George; almost at the same time, the daughter, recently married to a Frenchman, M. de Saint-Bérain, brought into the world a son who was called Agénor. It was this Agénor who, forty years later, appeared so surprisingly before the Député Barsac.

Five years later Lord Blazon had a second son, Lewis Robert, who, thirty-five years later, was unhappily involved in the affair of the Central Bank.

This great good fortune, to have a second child to carry on his name, was accompanied by the most dreadful of blows. The child's birth cost the life of his mother, and Lord Blazon saw the last of the one who, for more than a quarter of a century, had been his companion.

Struck by so cruel a blow, he staggered. Distressed and disheartened, he gave up his ambitions, and although still relatively young, he abandoned the Navy, in which he had served so long, and in which he might have attained the highest rank.

For long, following on this great misfortune, he lived withdrawn within himself; then, time having lessened his grief, he tried, after nine years of solitude, to reconstitute his broken household. He married the widow of one of his comrades, Marguerite Ferney, who brought him as her sole dowry a son, William, then aged sixteen.

But fate had decided that Lord Glenor should grow old alone, and that he should come alone to the end of his days. A few years later, a fourth child was born to him, a daughter who was called Jane, and he was widowed for the second time.

Lord Glenor was then over sixty years old, and at such an age he could no longer hope to rebuild his life. So cruelly, so inexorably struck down in his dearest affections, he devoted himself exclusively to his duty as a father. If his first daughter, now Madame de Saint-Bérain, had long been beyond his control, he still had four children, of whom the oldest was barely twenty, left to him by the two deaths, for in his heart he did not distinguish between William Ferney and the two sons and the daughter of his own blood.

But destiny had not yet relented, and the Lord of Glenor was still to know a sorrow compared with which those which had already smitten him seemed light.

The first blow which the future had in store for him came direct from William Ferney, his dead wife's son, whom he had cared for as one of his own. Sly, surly, indeed something of a hypocrite, the young man failed to respond to the kindness given him, and remained lonely in the midst of the family which had offered him its home and heart. He remained indifferent to the tokens of affection showered upon him. Indeed, the more interest shown him the more he withdrew fiercely; the more friendship was offered him, the greater seemed his hatred for those around him.

Envy, exasperated envy, wrathful envy, devoured his heart. He had felt this contemptible emotion from the very day on which he and his mother had entered Glenor Castle. Brooding over the difference between his own status and that of his two brothers, he conceived a violent hatred for George and Lewis, Lord Blazon's heirs; they would be rich, whereas he, the son of Margaret Ferney, would always be disinherited.

His hatred grew more intense at the birth of his half-sister, Jane, for she too would share one day in that fortune from which he was debarred, and of which he received, as though in charity, only a vestige. His hatred passed all bounds when his mother died and he lost the only one who might have found a way into his perverted heart.

Nothing appeased him, neither the brotherly friendship of

Lord Blazon's two sons, nor the fatherly solicitude of that nobleman. Every day he withdrew still further, leading a life whose secrets were revealed only by a series of scandals.

He was known to associate with evil companions, and to choose his friends from the least desirable of London's inhabitants.

The rumour of his excesses reached the ears of Lord Blazon, who wore himself out in vain in useless remonstrances. At last the debts which he had previously paid in tribute to his wife's memory became so great that he had to put an end to it.

Placed on a suitable allowance, William Ferney made no change in his way of life. It was a mystery how he obtained the necessary funds until there was presented at Glenor a draft for a large sum of money on which Lord Blazon's signature was very cleverly forged.

He paid it without saying a word. Then, refusing to tolerate a forger, he called the culprit to him and drove him from his presence, none the less promising him an adequate pension.

William Ferney listened with his usual air of cunning to reproaches and advice. Then, without saying a word, without even touching the first instalment of his pension, he left Glenor Castle and was heard of no more.

What happened to him afterwards, Lord Blazon never knew. Never again did he have a word from him, and little by little, as time passed, the painful memory died away.

Fortunately, the true children of Lord Glenor gave him as much satisfaction as the outsider had brought him care. In the same time as this fellow had gone never to return, George, following the glorious tradition of his family, passed out with honours from the Royal Military Academy and took a commission in the army, seeking adventure in the colonies.

To the great regret of Lord Blazon, the second son, Lewis, had no military ambition, though otherwise he showed himself worthy of his affection. He was serious-minded and competent, and one could always rely on his integrity.

During the years following William's exit, while the memory

of his misdeeds died away, the life of the two young men followed a regular and logical course. Lewis obviously had a vocation for business. Entering the service of the Central Bank, he was greatly esteemed and climbed the hierarchical ladder of that immense House, of which it was generally thought that he would one day take control. George, transferred from one colony to another, was more of a man of action and won his promotion at the sword-point.

Lord Blazon might well think that a hostile fate had finished with him, and he could foresee the happiest vistas for his old age. Then a misfortune, more terrible even than those which had already assailed him, suddenly struck him down. But now he was injured not merely in his heart but in his honour, in that pure honour of Glenor whose name would now be smirched forever by the most abominable of treasons.

Even to-day, in spite of the lapse of time, there may still be memories of that terrible drama in which the oldest son of Lord Blazon was the leading actor.

George Blazon, seconded from the Army, had been placed at the service of an important exploration company. For two years he worked for that company's benefit, at the head of a semi-regular body which it had enlisted. He was in Ashanti when it was reported that he had suddenly turned his coat and was in open revolt against his own country.

The news arrived with the brutality of a thunderbolt—the news not only of the revolt but of its inevitable punishment. It simultaneously described the treachery of Captain Blazon and of his men, now transformed into adventurers, their robberies, their tyranny, the cruelties they inflicted, and the repression which followed so closely on the crime.

The newspapers described the drama as it proceeded. They noted its progress, they described the rebel band relentlessly pursued and retreating gradually before the forces sent against them. They related how Captain Blazon, driven with several of his companions into regions then included within the French zone of influence, had at last been caught up with near the village of Koubo, at the foot of the Hombori Mountains, and had been killed at the first volley.

The officer responsible for his death had since died of fever; but though the punishment he had inflicted had cost him his life, it had been speedy and final.

Though at last the episode was generally forgotten, there was at least one dwelling where its memory lingered. It was that of Lord Blazon.

Struck at the same time in his passionate love for his son and in what was dearer to him still, his honour, the Lord of Glenor did not flinch beneath it, and even the paleness of his face hardly betrayed his grief. Without asking one question, without uttering one word on the intolerable subject, he withdrew into a haughty solitude and a disdainful silence.

From that day he was never seen, as of old, taking his daily walk. From that day, in the house from which even his oldest friends were debarred, he remained continually, hardly moving, silent, alone.

Alone? Not altogether. There were three who in turn stayed with him, finding in the respect they felt for him the courage to support that frightful existence with a living statue, with a ghost, who though still in bodily form had locked himself of his own free will in an eternal silence.

First there was his second son, Lewis Robert Blazon, who did not let a week pass without spending his one free day at Glenor Castle.

There was also his grandson, Agénor de Saint-Bérain, who tried to lighten by his cheerful good-humour the claustral sadness of the household.

Though, when George Blazon committed his incredible treachery, Agénor corresponded in every detail with the somewhat unflattering description given by the orderly, he was none the less a splendid fellow, helpful and obliging, tender-hearted, and with an unshakable loyalty.

In three details he differed from others: an incredible absent-mindedness; a passion beyond all bounds—and sometimes very unfortunate—for angling; and above all, a fierce dislike for female company.

A competence inherited from his parents having made him independent, he had left France at the first tidings of the disaster which had felled his grandfather, and had settled in a villa near Glenor Castle, where he spent most of his time.

Its garden was traversed by a stream, and into this Agénor plunged his fishing-lines with an enthusiasm as compelling as it was inexplicable. Why was he so keen on that pastime when he was always thinking of something else, and when all the fishes in the world could "bite" without his noticing how his float was bobbing? And even if a barbel, a roach, or a pike, even more impetuous than his captor was absent-minded, had deliberately hooked itself, how would that have helped the compassionate Agénor, who would no doubt have thrown it back into the water at once, perhaps even begging its pardon?

A fine fellow, as we have explained.

But what a woman-hater! He would explain his dislike of the sex to anyone who would listen to him. He credited them with all the faults, all the vices. "Deceitful, perfidious, liars, spendthrifts," he proclaimed them to be, not to mention the other epithets for which he was never at a loss.

When anyone advised him to get married; "Me!" he would exclaim, "me, to ally myself with one of those faithless robbers!"

And, if he were pressed : "I shall never believe in a woman's love," he would say quite seriously, "until I see her die of grief upon my tomb."

This result being difficult to achieve, the odds were that he would remain a bachelor.

His dislike for the fair sex permitted only one exception. The privilege was extended to Jane Blazon, last of the children of the Lord of Glenor, and in consequence Agénor's aunt, but an aunt fifteen years younger than himself, an aunt whom he had known from infancy, whose first steps he had guided, and of whom he became the guardian from the time when the unfortunate nobleman shunned the world. He felt an almost fatherly tenderness for her, a deep affection which she reciprocated. In theory he was her teacher, but a teacher who did all he could to become her disciple. They hardly ever parted. They went about together, roaming the woods on foot or on horseback, boating, hunting, following different kinds of sport, until the elderly nephew felt able to say about his young aunt, whom he brought up as a tomboy, that he would end by making a man of her!

Jane Blazon was the third to care for the aged nobleman, watching over his distress with almost a motherly love. She would have given her life to make him smile, and her hope of bringing a little happiness into her father's embittered soul never left her. This was the only aim of all her thoughts, of everything she did.

She realized at once that her father was weeping not so much for the miserable end of a son subjected to just retribution as for his tarnished name and his violated honour. She, on the other hand, did not weep.

Not that she did not feel the loss of her dearly-loved brother and the stain upon the family escutcheon. But even stronger than grief was the protest of her heart. What! Lewis and her father to believe so readily in George's disgrace! Without checking it, without making any enquiry, they accepted as proved these accusations from far beyond the seas! What mattered the official reports? Against these reports, against the evidence itself, the whole history of George rose in protest. That he should be a traitor—her splendid brother, so upright, so good, so pure, whose whole life bore witness to his heroism and loyalty—that was unthinkable! Let the whole world disown him, she at least would honour his memory, and her faith in him should never fail.

Time served only to strengthen her belief. As the days passed, the firmer grew her conviction in her brother's innocence although there was no evidence to support it. The moment at last came, several years after the event, when she dared for the first time to break the absolute silence which, by tacit agreement, everyone in the castle maintained about the tragedy of Koubo.

"Uncle?" she said one day, in an interrogative voice, to Agénor de St. Bérain.

Although he was really her nephew, they usually reversed, in practice, the order of their relationship, so as to bring it more into line with their respective ages. This was why Agénor usually called Jane his niece, and she bestowed upon him the title of uncle; this was almost always so. ...

Not always, however.

If it happened by chance that this so-called uncle gave his pseudo-niece any reason for complaint, or if he tried to resist her wishes, or even one of her whims, she would at once revert to her true status and indicate to her "nephew" that he ought to show proper respect to his "elders". Realizing the position, the "nephew" hastened to sing small and to appease his venerable "aunt." This clash of titles sometimes gave rise to remarkable dialogues.

"Uncle?" Jane asked that day.

"Yes, dear?" replied Agénor, lost in a treatise on angling.

"I want to talk about George."

Agénor was so startled that he put his book down.

"About George?" he asked, somewhat perturbed. "What George?"

"About my brother George," Jane informed him calmly.

Agénor grew pale. "But you know," he protested in a trembling voice, "that this name must not be spoken here."

Jane repulsed the objection with a movement of her head.

"That doesn't matter," she said quietly. "Tell me about George, uncle."

"What do you want me to tell you?"

"Everything about him—everything."

"That I never will!"

Jane frowned.

"Nephew!" she said in menacing tones.

Nothing more was needed.

"All right! All right" babbled Agénor, and he began to relate the sad story.

He related it in full detail. Jane listened in silence and did not ask any more questions. Thinking the matter was settled, Agénor heaved a sigh of relief.

He was mistaken. A few days later, Jane returned to the charge.

"Uncle?" she asked again.

"Yes, dear?"

"Suppose George wasn't guilty?"

Agénor could hardly believe his ears.

"Not guilty?" he repeated. "I'm sorry to say, my poor child, that there's no doubt about it. The wretched fellow—his guilt and his death are historic facts, proved up to the hilt."

"How?" Jane asked.

Agénor went over the ground again. He cited the articles in the papers, the official reports against which nobody had protested. Finally he invoked the absence of the accused—a definite proof of his death.

"Of his death, yes," Jane objected, "but hardly of his treachery."

"The one was the result of the other," Agénor replied, her obstinacy putting him at a loss.

This obstinacy was even greater than he supposed. From that day onward she often returned to the painful subject, harassing Agénor with continual questions. From these he readily inferred that she still had faith in her brother's innocence.

On this point, however, Agénor remained unmoved. In response to her best arguments, he contented himself with shaking his head sadly like a man who wished to avoid a useless discussion; Jane realized that his belief was not to be shaken.

One day she lost patience and decided to put her foot down.

"Uncle?" she began again.

"Yes, dear?" he replied as usual.

"I've been thinking things over, Uncle, and I've come to the conclusion that George is innocent."

"But, my dear," Agénor began.

"There's no 'but' about it," Jane cut him short. "Uncle, George is innocent."

"Yet . . ."

Jane got up, her nostrils quivering. "I tell you, my nephew," she said grimly, "my brother George is innocent."

Agénor gave in.

"So he is, Aunt," he agreed, humbly.

Since then, George's innocence had been an acknowledged fact, and Agénor de St. Bérain never let himself dispute it. Moreover, Jane's certainty was not without some effect on his own mind. If he did not share her convictions of the recreant captain's innocence, at least they shook his belief in the reality of his guilt.

In the years that followed, Jane's thoughts kept developing in the direction of a faith which, however ardent, was sentimental rather than reasoned. To have gained a fellow-believer was indeed something, but not very much. What was the use of announcing the innocence of her brother when she could not prove it? And how was she to get any proof? At last she felt she had thought out a method.

"It's understood then," she said one day to Agénor, "that George is innocent?"

"Yes dear," replied Agénor, who none the less did not feel too certain about it.

"He was far too intelligent," Jane continued, "to do anything so stupid, and too proud to degrade himself. He loved his country too much to betray it."

"That's clear enough."

"We've lived with him. I understood his thoughts as well as I do my own. He had no other motive than honour, no other love than for our father, no other ambition than the glory of our country. And you will have it that he had the idea of betraying it, of dishonouring it by turning filibuster, of covering himself and his family with shame? Tell me! That's how you want to have it, Agénor?"

"Me! I don't want anything, Aunt," protested Agénor, thinking it more prudent to make use of that respectful title.

"And you sit there, staring at me with those great round eyes, as if you'd never seen me before! You know quite well that so abominable an idea could never have entered his head! Well, if that's what you know, say it!"

"I say it, Aunt, I do say it!"

"That's not so bad! But as for those who invented that story, they are wretches."

"Villains."

"They ought to be sent to jail."

"Or hung."

"Along with the journalists whose lying stories brought us despair and shame!"

"Yes, all the journalists! They ought to be hung! They ought to be shot!"

"You feel quite sure of that!"

"Absolutely!"

"Well, I wanted to make sure you didn't doubt it!"

"Never have I thought. . . ."

"Good! If it wasn't for that, understand me, I'd have driven you from my presence and never set eyes on you again."

"Heaven preserve me!" cried poor Agénor, greatly alarmed by this terrible threat.

Jane paused and glanced at her victim out of the corner of her eye. Certainly she had thought things out, for she modified her violence in a way less sincere than calculated, and said more quietly, "It isn't enough for the two of us to believe in George's innocence. We must find some way of proving it, Uncle dear, as you will see."

Agénor's face lighted up. The storm must have passed.

"That's clear," he agreed, with a sigh of relief.

"Without that we could shout from the housetops that George is not guilty, but nobody would believe us."

"That's only too certain, my poor dear."

"When my father himself—his own father!—accepts the truth of a few rumours which began nobody knows where, when he's dying of grief and shame under our very eyes, without having repulsed these abominable rumour-mongers, when he did not at once exclaim 'You're lying! George could never commit such a crime!' how can I expect to convince strangers without giving clear proofs of my brother's innocence?"

"That's as clear as daylight," agreed Agénor, stroking his chin. "But there we are. . . . Those proofs . . . where are we to find them?"

"Not here, that's plain." Jane paused, then added quietly, "Somewhere else, perhaps."

"Somewhere else? Where, my dear child?"

"Where the thing occured. At Koubo."

"At Koubo!"

"Yes, at Koubo. There they can first find George's grave, because it was there that they say he died, and if so, there they can see how he died. Then they can hunt out the survivors—the troop he commanded was sizeable, and they can't all have vanished. These witnesses, they can question them, and so bring the truth to light."

As Jane spoke, her face lit up, and her voice trembled with enthusiasm.

"You're quite right, little one," cried Agénor, naïvely falling into the trap.

Jane put on her stubborn look. "Well," she said, "if I'm right, someone must go there."

"Where?" asked Agénor, startled.

"Where . . . to Koubo, Uncle."

"To Koubo? And who the devil do you want to send to Koubo?"

Jane threw her arms about his neck.

"You, Uncle dear," she murmured sweetly.

"Me!"

Agénor freed himself. For once he was really annoyed.

"You're crazy!" he replied, trying to get away.

"Not so very crazy!" replied Jane, holding him back. "And why, if you please, shouldn't you go to Koubo? Don't you like travelling?"

"I hate it. Having to be in time to catch a train, that's more than I can do."

"And you hate fishing too, don't you?"

"Fishing? I don't see what you're getting at?"

"What do you say to fried fish—caught in the Niger? That would be something out of the way! In the Niger, where the gudgeons are the size of sharks, and the minnows are like tunny! And you won't even try it!"

"I didn't say.... However...."

"And while you were fishing you could make your enquiries, you could ask the natives...."

"In what language?" Agénor chaffed her. "I didn't know those coconuts spoke English!"

Jane did not look amused. "That's why it would be better to ask them in Bambara."

"In Bambara? Am I supposed to know Bambara?"

"Well, you can learn it."

"At my age?"

"Well, I've learned it, and I'm your aunt."

"You? Can you speak Bambara?"

"Certainly. Just listen to this: *'Dfi lokho a bé na'*."

"Whatever's that gibberish?"

"That means 'I'm thirsty.' And *'I dou, nono i mita.'*"

"I swear... *nono... mita.*"

"That means, 'Come in, I'll give you some milk.' And *'Koukho bé na. Kounou ouarara uté a man doumouni.'* Don't rack your brains. Translation: 'I'm very hungry, I've eaten nothing since yesterday morning.'"

"And I've got to learn *that?*"

"Yes, and a good deal more. And don't lose any time about it, for we'll soon have to be off."

"What do you mean, be off? Because I'm not going, for one. What an idea! No, I can't see myself hob-nobbing with your savages."

Jane seemed to give up hope of persuading him. "Then I shall have to go by myself," she said sadly.

"By yourself!" bleated Agénor, astonished. "You want to go by yourself."

"To Koubo? Certainly."

"A thousand miles inland?"

"Over eleven hundred, my dear Uncle."

"Face dangers like that! And by yourself?"

"I shall have to, if you won't come with me," Jane answered dryly.

"It's madness! It's absolute lunacy! It's *delirium tremens*," cried Agénor, who saw that the only thing to do was to dash out and slam the door.

But when he wanted to talk to Jane next day, she refused to reply or pay attention, and so it went on for the next few days. Agénor wasn't strong enough to play that game. In four days he had to strike his flag.

Thenceforward, whenever his young aunt suggested anything, he gradually came to share her views. That journey, which he had first regarded as crazy, he thought next day to be dangerous, the third day feasible, and the fourth day quite easy.

That was why, within four times twenty-four hours, he had apologized handsomely, admitted his error, and declared himself ready to set out.

Jane was generous enough not to hold him to that.

"First you've got to learn the language," she said, kissing him on both cheeks.

From that time on, whenever one saw Agénor he was poring over a Bambara grammar.

Before setting off, however, Jane had to make certain that

her father agreed. She obtained his consent much more easily than she had dared hope. Hardly had she mentioned, without going into details, her plan for undertaking the voyage when he made a gesture of assent, only to plunge once again into his habitual sadness. Had he as much as heard her? So far as could be seen, nothing now interested him.

That settled, Jane and Agénor began getting ready for their journey. Not then realizing the help the Barsac Mission was to give them, they had to act as if they would be alone, and with only their own resources, to undertake that crazy peregrination of more than two thousand miles.

For several years Jane had carefully studied the geography of the countries she had to pass through. The works of such explorers as Captain Binger had described in full detail the regions and its inhabitants.

Thus she learned that if she attempted an armed exploration, surrounded by a regiment of several hundred volunteers, whom she would have to arm, feed, and pay, she would first of all incur considerable expense. She would, moreover, be hurling herself against a warlike population who would oppose by force an incursion made by force. She would then have to fight in order to attain her end, even assuming she could attain it at all.

Captain Binger indeed declared that if the natives wished they could stop any expedition, either by attacking it or by devastating the country and starving it out.

Much impressed by this statement, Jane had decided to attempt a peaceful journey. Hardly any visible weapons, a few devoted trustworthy men, and the sinews of war represented not only by money but by presents for the village chiefs and their headmen.

After having designed linen garments for the dry weather, and thick woollen ones for the rainy season, Jane and Agénor packed them in light cases, restricting these to the smallest possible number. Then they crated up gifts for the natives: second-rate secondhand guns, gaudy or variegated cloth, silk and cotton handkerchiefs, glass pearls, needles, pins, haberdashery, lace, buttons, pencils, and so forth, the whole trumpery of a bazaar.

They took also or themselves a small chemist's shop, weapons, telescopes, compasses, camp equipment, dictionaries and a few other books, the most up-to-date maps, cooking utensils, toilet materials, tea, provisions, indeed a whole carefully-selected cargo of objects essential for a long stay in the bush, far from any centre of supply.

Finally a metal case, made of nickel which sparkled in the sun, contained a selection of fishing-rods, lines and hooks, enough for half-a-dozen anglers. That was Agénor's personal luggage.

The aunt and the nephew—or the uncle and niece, whichever you prefer—would then set off for Liverpool, where they would embark for the African coast. Their first intention was to start from the British colony of Gambia, and it was not until they learned, when stopping at St. Louis, that a French Mission was waiting at Konakry, and that it meant to follow a route similar to their own, that they decided to join the compatriots of St. Bérain.

Towards the end of September they sent to Liverpool their multifarious luggage, and on the 2nd October they had their last meal together, for Lord Blazon never left his room, in the great dining-hall of Glenor Castle. In spite of the grandeur of the task she had imposed on herself, Jane Blazon could not refrain from thinking that perhaps she would never again see this castle, the cradle of her infancy and youth, and that when she returned, if she ever returned, her old father might no longer be there to welcome her to his arms.

And yet it was above all for him that she was embarking on this adventure, so full of danger and effort. It was to bring a little happiness to his desolate heart that she was going to rehabilitate his name, to efface the stain which had smirched his escutcheon.

As the hour for departure approached, Jane asked her

father to let them say good-bye, and was ushered, along with Agénor, into the old man's room. He was sitting near the great window which looked out on the countryside. His eyes seemed fixed on the remote distance, as if he were waiting for someone to come into sight. Who could it be? George his son— George the traitor?

On hearing his daughter, he turned his head slightly and his dim eye brightened. But it was only a gleam. His eyelids fell; his face resumed its customary lack of expression.

"Good-bye, Father," said Jane, striving to keep back her tears.

Lord Glenor did not reply. Rising from his arm-chair, he grasped the hand of the young girl; then, pressing her gently against him, he bestowed a kiss on her forehead.

For fear of bursting into sobs, Jane withdrew from his grasp and went away in tears.

The old man then seized Agénor's hand, shook it, and, as if to demand his protection, gestured towards the door through which Jane had just vanished.

"Rely on me," Agénor assured him.

Then Lord Blazon resumed his former attitude, and his glance was once more lost in the depths of the landscape, while, strongly moved, St. Bérain left him.

A carriage was waiting for them in the courtyard of the castle, to take them to Uttoxeter station, about two miles away.

"Where to now?" asked the incorrigible Agénor, who, still distressed by the visit he had just made, did not quite realize that they were leaving Glenor.

Jane contented herself with shrugging her shoulders, and they set out.

But scarcely had they gone five hundred yards when St. Bérain, suddenly became amazingly agitated. He could not speak, he seemed to be choking. "My lines! My lines!" he exclaimed at last in a heart-rending voice.

They had to return to the castle to look for the famous

fishing-lines which he had forgotten, and this lost them a good quarter of an hour. When they arrived at the station, the express was in. The travellers only just had time to get aboard, and this made Agénor say, not without a certain vanity: "This is only the second time in my life that I haven't lost the train."

Jane could not help smiling through her tears, which were still flowing freely.

Thus began a journey which would lead the two explorers into the unknown. Would Jane have undertaken it if she had known what would take place during her absence? Would she have left her unfortunate father if she had suspected the blow which was just about to strike him—just as she was risking her life to save him from despair?

No, nothing could have enabled her to foresee the tragedy which was about to take place in the offices of the Central Bank, nor the infamous accusation of which her brother Lewis would be the object; thinking to help her father, she had left him just at the very moment when her help was needed nearer home.

Brought by too zealous a servant, the news of the disappearance of Robert Lewis Blazon came to the Lord of Glenor on the morning which followed the crime at Old Broad Street. The shock felled him. This descendant of a long line of heroes, this fierce devotee of honour, now learned that of his two sons, not only was one a traitor but the other was a thief!

The wretched old man uttered a stifled groan, clutched at his throat, and dropped on the floor.

The servants crowded around him. They lifted him up. They lavished attentions upon him until at last he opened his eyes.

The look of those eyes was thenceforward the only sign that life had not completely left his stricken heart. If he should live, his body, struck by paralysis, would be condemned to eternal stillness. But even that was not enough to appease the cruelty of fate. Senseless, dumb, inert, Lord Blazon could still think!

And, allowing for the difference in longitude, it was just when her father fell senseless that Jane Blazon, aided by Captain Marcenay, put her foot in the stirrup, and, crossing the bridge which unites Konakry to the continent, really began her travels and took the first step into the mysteries of Darkest Africa.

CHAPTER IV

AN ARTICLE FROM *L'ÉXPANSION FRANÇAISE*

ON THE first of January the readers of *L'Éxpansion Française* could enjoy the following article. It had a displayed title and it came from the somewhat fantastic pen—it is easy to romance about what is far away!—of their able reporter, M. Amédée Florence, whose readers would willingly excuse its somewhat familiar style :

THE BARSAC MISSION

(From our special correspondent)

In the Bush, 1st December. As I have already explained, the Barsac Mission is to set out to-day at six in the morning. At that hour we are all ready, including two volunteers who have come to join the eight members—official as much as officious —whom we know already. Nobody grumbles at that! One of these volunteers is indeed a ravishing young lady, a Frenchwoman, educated in England, from which she has derived a slight and very agreeable accent. Mademoiselle Jane Mornas, that's her name. The other volunteer, her uncle—provided he isn't her nephew, for we needn't get mixed up in these questions of relationship—is called Agénor de Saint-Bérain. He is an eccentric whose vagaries, already a byword in Konakry, make us hope for some cheerful moments.

Mlle Mornas and M. de Saint-Bérain are travelling for their pleasure. I should be lacking in any sense of gallantry if I did not add—and for ours. They have brought with them two black servants, formerly Senegalese Tirailleurs, who will act as guides rather than as interpreters, for our two globe-trotters speak enough Bambara and several other local dialects. Mlle Mornas, in particular, has a way of greeting us with an *Initié* (good-morning)! . . . I need say no more !

M. Barsac has taken up the word and repeats it at every opportunity, but on his lips it hasn't the same charm.

So, this morning, the first of December, about half past five, here we are assembled on the square of Konakry, before the Residency.

As I explained before, M. Barsac wants to make a peaceful and exclusively civil expedition. As optimistic here as at the tribune of the Chamber, he thinks he has only to appear before the people, olive-branch in hand, in order to turn a march beside the Niger, from Konakry to Kotonou, into a mere constitutional. This is also the idea of Mlle Mornas, who is nervous of frightening the natives by too great a display of force.

But the Barsac-Mornas party has run up against the opposition of the Baudrières party. The Associate-Chief of the Mission—a man who never seems to smile—paints a dark picture of the dangers we are about to run. He speaks of the dignity of a Mission headed by two representatives of the French people and of the prestige we gain from an escort of regular soldiers; and, to our surprise, he is supported by the Governor, M. Valdonne.

Without disputing that French penetration has largely pacified the black country, the Governor repeats what the Minister for the Colonies has already maintained in the Chamber. M. Valdonne tells us that there are facts, mysterious or at least unexplained, which prompt the fear that some uprising is being plotted. It seems that, for about ten years and to a greater extent recently, more especially in the Niger region from Say to Djenne, whole villages have been suddenly abandoned and that their inhabitants have vanished, and that other villages have been pillaged and burned—by whom nobody knows. In all, these rumours tend to indicate that something—nobody knows quite what—is afoot in the shadows.

The most elementary prudence therefore compels the Mission to have an armed escort. This consideration has prevailed,

AN ARTICLE FROM L'ÉXPANSION FRANÇAISE 63

to the great satisfaction of M. Baudrières, and M. Barsac has to resign himself to the protection of Captain Marcenay and his two hundred cavalrymen.

At six o'clock, all is ready. The convoy forms up under the direction of a negro who has already made the journey from Konakry to Sikasso several times, and who is to be our guide. He is a good fellow of thirty, formerly a *dougoukoussadigui* (native officer). He wears longcloth breeches and an old colonial infantryman's tunic with torn and filthy stripes. If his feet are bare, his head, on the contrary, is covered with a linen helmet that once was white decorated with a superb tricolour plume. For emblem of office, he has a thick cudgel by which he can make himself understood by the porters and the muleteers.

Immediately behind him comes Mlle Mornas, escorted by M. Barsac and Captain Marcenay. Well, well! they do not seem oblivious of the young lady's attractions. I should bet that during the journey there's going to be some rivalry. Your readers may rest assured that I'll keep them in touch with the developments of that contest.

M. Baudrières follows that first group, smartly turned out— did I say we're all on horseback?—but his severe look seems to disapprove of his colleague's showing so plainly how much our amiable companion is to his taste. I glance at him, this Associate-Chief, out of the corner of my eye. How thin he is! and cold! and sad! . . . Why, confound it, he doesn't seem to know what smiling is.

Three paces behind the Honourable Deputy from the Nord come the others. Dr. Châtonnay and the geographer are discussing ethnography—already.

The convoy, correctly so called, comes behind them. It consists of fifty donkeys led by twenty-five muleteers, of whom ten really belong to Mlle Mornas and M. de St. Bérain. On the flanks are Captain Marcenay's cavalrymen. As for your humble servant, he makes it his task to canter along the column from one end to the other.

Tchoumouki and Tongané, Mlle Mornas' two servants, form the rearguard.

Exactly at six comes the signal to start. The column moves off. At that moment the Tricolour Flag rises over the Residency—I beg pardon! Let us use some local colour: over the *Case* of the Governor who, in full uniform to suit the occasion, gives us a farewell salute from the height of his balcony. The bugles and drums of the local section of the Colonial Infantry sound and beat the military honours. We raise our hats. The moment is somewhat solemn, and—you may laugh—I confess that my eyes are moist.

Why must so solemn an occasion be interrupted by a piece of nonsense?

St. Bérain? Where's St. Bérain? St. Bérain has been forgotten! We look for him, we call him. The echoes repeat his name. It's all in vain. St. Bérain does not reply.

We begin to fear some mishap. But Mlle Mornas, who does not seem uneasy, reassures us.

No, Mlle Mornas is not uneasy. My word, she is furious!

"I'll fetch St. Bérain in three minutes," she says between her clenched teeth.

She claps spurs to her horse.

First, however, she's found time to turn towards me and say, "Monsieur Florence . . ." with a little pleading expression which I understand quite well. That's why I also use my spurs and ride off after her.

A few strides take us to the shore, facing the open sea—no doubt you know that Konakry is on an island—and there, what do I see?

M. de St. Bérain. Yes, ladies and gentlemen, St. Bérain as large as life, like you or me.

What's he doing there? We pause for a moment to find out.

M. de St. Bérain is comfortably seated on the sand, and doesn't seem to have any idea that he's holding up an official Mission. He is amiably chatting with a negro who is showing him some fish-hooks, probably of a type unknown in Europe, and is explaining them at great length. Then they both get up and walk towards a canoe half drawn up on the shore in which the negro embarks. . . . Heaven forgive me! M. de St. Bérain, doesn't he look like getting into it himself?

He doesn't get the chance.

"Nephew!" Mlle Mornas suddenly calls in severe tones.

(Certainly he is her nephew).

That word is enough. M. de St. Bérain turns round and sees his aunt—for his aunt she must be. Apparently the sight refreshes his memory, for he gives an exclamation of despair, lifts his arms heavenwards, throws his black friend a handful of money, grabs in return a batch of fish-hooks, thrusts them pell-mell into his pocket, and runs headlong towards us.

He's so funny that we roar with laughter. This enables Mlle Mornas to disclose a double row of dazzling white teeth. Dazzling, I repeat!

We turn about and M. de St. Bérain trots alongside our horses. But Mlle Mornas takes pity on the poor man; slowing her pace to a walk, she says gently: "Don't run like that, Uncle. You'll get over-heated."

(He's her uncle, then? . . . Oh! my head!)

We regain the convoy, where we are welcomed with ironical smiles. M. de St. Bérain doesn't worry about such trifles. He merely seems surprised to find so many people about.

"Am I late, then?" he asks innocently.

At this the whole column begins to laugh, and M. de St. Bérain joins in. I can't help liking the fellow.

But we haven't got away yet.

Just as M. de St. Bérain bends down, like the good horseman he is, to see that his saddle-girths are properly adjusted, the case for his fishing-lines, which he is wearing like a bandolier, unluckily bumps against the flank of one of the donkeys. The animal is skittish. It lets fly a kick at the unfortunate St. Bérain, who rolls in the dust.

We all rush to his help. But the good fellow is already up.

"That's very good! Mossoo have much luck," Tongané tells

him. "If bee sting or horse give kick, good journey, very fine."

Without answering him, M. de St. Bérain, dispirited and covered with dust, jumps into the saddle, and at last the convoy can be off.

By this time the sun has risen, and its first gleams are cheerfully lighting our route.

The path we are to follow, after crossing the bridge joining Konakry to the mainland, is fairly good. It is quite a road, five or six yards wide, along which a vehicle can easily pass, that we are to follow as far as Timbo, about 250 miles. Thus, until we reach Timbo at any rate, we need expect no serious difficulty.

For the rest, the weather is good, the temperature is agreeable—barely 50° in the shade—and we need not fear those terrible tropical downpours, for the rainy season is over.

Come on! All is for the best in the best of possible worlds.

About ten we cross a bridge over a stream of water which M. Tassin says is an affluent of the Manea, or else of the Morebayah, unless it's one or other of them. At present we are still in a cruel state of incertitude about this.

Anyhow, crossing rivers is the small change of travel in this part of Africa. There isn't a day, so to speak, on which one doesn't have to cross at least one of them. Understand then, as my articles aren't a course in geography, that I shall not talk about this exercise, unless it should be out of the ordinary in some way.

Near Konakry the route follows almost a straight line across a countryside but little diversified by hills. It is bordered by fields, fairly well cultivated. Maize or millet, with a few clumps of trees: cotton-trees, bananas, and so forth. We come across a few scattered insignificant hamlets, to which M. Tassin gives names which I think he must have made up himself. So far as we can tell, however, they might just as well be authentic.

Towards ten it gets hot, and Captain Marcenay orders a

halt. We have come about twelve miles from Konakry, which is quite satisfactory. We are going to have lunch and rest; then, after another meal, we shall set off about five in the afternoon, and make camp for the night about nine this evening.

This is to be our programme every day, so I shall not mention it again. Naturally I do not mean to weary my readers with trifling details of our journey. I take a lofty view of things, and I'll jot them down in my note-book only when they are remarkable in some way or other.

That explained, let's get on.

The halting place has been admirably chosen by Captain Marcenay. We have settled down in the shade of a little wood which will shelter us fairly well against the heat of the sun. While the soldiers scatter we—I mean the members of the Mission, Mlle Mornas, the Captain, M. de St. Bérain and your humble servant—we, I say, take our places in a pleasant clearing.

I offer a cushion to our fair companion, but Captain Marcenay and M. Barsac have forestalled me, and have each brought a camp-stool. What embarrassment! Mlle Mornas does not know which to choose. Already the captain and the leader of the Mission are looking somewhat askance at one another. Mlle Mornas brings them into accord by sitting on the ground—on my cushion. The two aspirants cast angry glances at me.

M. Baudrières sits to one side on a little clump of grass, in the midst of a group formed of those whom I call the "neutrals." They are the more or less competent delegates of the various ministries, Mm. Heyrieux, Quirieu, and Poncin.

The last-named, the most remarkable of the three, has not ceased to make notes since we started. I do not know, indeed, what they are. If he were less "official" I would hint that he marvellously suggests the character of M. Prud'homme[1]. What

[1] A semi-fictional character, a stuffy and somewhat sententious member of the *bourgeoisie*.—I.O.E.

a brow! With such a forehead, one must be either wondrously intelligent or outstandingly dull. Nothing in between. In which category must I place M. Poncin? I don't know.

Dr. Châtonnay and M. Tassin, so inseparable that they remind us of a couple of love-birds, take up a position under a fig tree. They are spreading geographical maps on the ground. I hope that they are not going to make them their only food.

Moriliré, who is certainly making himself useful, has brought us a table and a form. I sit down while reserving a place for M. de St. Bérain.

But M. de St. Bérain isn't there! What's more, M. de St. Bérain is never there!

Moriliré gets a camp-kitchen ready. Assisted by Tchoumouki and Tongané, he is going to do the cooking, for we have decided not to use more than we can help of the provisions we've brought from Europe. These are to be reserved on the chance—which should be unlikely—that we shan't be able to get enough fresh food by living on the country.

He bought some meat at Konakry. He shows it to us:

"Me make it fine stew with *sadé* (lamb)," he tells us, "tender as a baby."

Tender as a baby! That comparison makes our flesh creep. Has Moriliré ever tasted human flesh, we wonder? We ask him. He tells us, in rather hypocritical tones, that he's never eaten it himself, but he's heard its exquisite savour praised highly. H'm!

Our first meal doesn't recall the Café Anglais, but all the same it's excellent. Judge for yourself: quarters of lamb grilled with millet paste and sauce made of Karité butter, a salad, a maize cake, figs, bananas, and coconut. Washed down by the pure water of a stream which flows at our feet, and, for those who like it, palm-tree wine.

These dishes are preceded by an hors-d'œuvre which our *maître-d'hôtel* had not foreseen. But let us not anticipate, as they say in well-constructed novelettes.

While Moriliré and his two assistants are preparing the meal, Dr. Châtonnay comes up and gives us some highly technical information regarding such local food-stuffs as Karité butter—also called Cé butter, for the tree from which it comes has two names. He explains how it is prepared.

"You know everything, Doctor," Mlle Mornas says admiringly.

"No, Mademoiselle, but I've read widely, especially the admirable works of Captain Binger."

This worthy doctor is still at it with his scientific explanations when my attention is drawn by cries coming from the wood. We at once recognize the voice which utters them.

I should bet that, if I ask my readers the simple question : "Whom does that voice belong to?" they would at once reply in chorus "I know! M. de St. Bérain!"

You readers are not mistaken. It is, indeed, M. de St. Bérain who is shouting for help.

I hasten to answer his call, followed by Captain Marcenay and M. Barsac. We find him in a marsh, sunk to his middle in the mud.

When we've got him on to dry land: "How did you fall into that marsh—or *marigot,* as they call it in this country?" I ask him.

"I slipped," he answered, spattering me with mud. "I slipped while I was fishing."

"With a line?"

"Not a bit of it. By hand, my dear fellow."

He shows us his colonial helmet wrapped in a fold of his jacket.

"Wait," he says, without giving me any other answer. "I must unwrap my jacket carefully, or they'll escape."

"What do you mean, they?"

"Frogs."

While we were relaxing, he has been fishing for frogs. What an enthusiast!

"I congratulate you," M. Barsac says approvingly. "They make good eating, frogs. . . . But listen to them croaking, the ones you've caught. It's clear they don't want to be eaten!"

At this we return to the camp. St. Bérain has a change of clothes and Moriliré cooks his "catch." The table being laid, we eat with the gusto of those who have swallowed twelve miles on horseback by way of an appetiser.

It goes without saying that Mlle Mornas presides. She's really delicious. (I've said so before, I know, but I can't repeat it too often.) A dear simple child, pleasantly boyish, she quickly puts us at our ease.

"My uncle. . . ." (Then he's really her uncle? Is that it?) "My uncle," she explains, "brought me up like a boy, and he's made a man of me. Please forget my sex, and think of me only as one of yourselves."

This does not keep her, even as she speaks, from giving Captain Marcenay one of those half-smiles, which show as plain as a pike-staff that, among this sort of boy, coquetry still has its place.

We take our coffee. After this, quietly stretched out in the long grass in the shade of the palm-trees, we give ourselves up to the joys of the siesta.

We were, as I explained, to set out at five; but when it's time for the convoy to form up, we come up against a brick wall, if I may use so strong an expression.

In vain Moriliré, when the time came, orders the men to get ready. To our great surprise they refuse, crying all at once that they haven't seen the moon, and that they can't go on because they haven't seen the moon!

We are bewildered, but our savant, M. Tassin, explains the mystery.

"I know just what it is," he tells us. "All the explorers have mentioned it in the records of their journeys. When the moon is new—this evening it is only two days old—the negroes always say 'That's a bad sign. Nobody has seen the moon yet. The road won't be good for us'."

"*Ioo! Ioo!*" ("Yes! yes!") comes the noisy approval of the muleteers and porters who are grouped round us, when Moriliré has translated the words of the geographical doctor. "*Karo! Karo!*" ("The moon! The Moon!").

It seems certain that, if the satellite continues in its refusal to show itself, these blockheads will continue in their refusal to move off. And it's still day, and the sky is hidden.

Certainly, these gentlemen of colour had made up their minds, and perhaps we should be there yet if, a little before six, the pale crescent of the moon had not appeared between two clouds. The blacks utter cries of delight.

"*Allah ma toula kendé*," they say, touching their foreheads with their right hands. "*Karo koutayé*." ("God has been good to us; we can see the new moon.")

At once the column sets off without difficulty.

But we have lost two hours, and the evening's march must be shortened accordingly.

About nine, we halt in the midst of the bush, and the tents are pitched. The country is not completely deserted, however. To the right of the footpath is a native hut, abandoned for some reason; on our left we can see another, but this seems to be inhabited.

Captain Marcenay looks into the former, and judging it fairly tolerable, suggests that Mlle Mornas should make it her home for the night. She accepts and vanishes into this unexpected hostelry.

Hardly has she gone ten minutes when we hear her calling loudly for help. We dash across and find her standing in front of the hut and pointing disgustedly to its floor.

"What's this?" she asks.

"This" consists of countless white maggots. They have come out of the earth and are writhing about in such numbers that the very soil seemed to be heaving.

"Just think, gentlemen," says Mlle Mornas, "how frightened I was when I felt their cold touch on my face, on my hands! I found them everywhere, even in my pockets! When I shook myself they kept falling out of my clothing. Ugh! The ugly beasts!"

M. de St. Bérain comes up at that moment, and finds the suitable word without any trouble.

"Oh look," he exclaims, his face lighting up, "they are gentles!"

And indeed they must have been gentles, for he knows all about them, does M. de St. Bérain.

Already he's bending down to get a supply of them.

"You no need for that," Tongané tells him. "There's plenty where we go. Them very bad, grow everywhere. No way kill them."

There's something that promises us some pleasant nights! But the natives, what do they do with these legions of maggots?

No doubt I was thinking out loud.

"Eat them, Mossoo," explains Tongané. "Them nice!"

Mlle Mornas, not sharing the simple tastes of the inhabitants of this country, was simply going to move into one of the tents when Moriliré tells her that a young negress, the servant of a farmer of the same colour who's away just now, is offering her hospitality in a hut. This is quite clean and—unlikely as it seems—is furnished with a bedstead of European type.

"You give money," the guide adds. "This good!"

Mlle Mornas accepts the proffered hospitality and we escort her ceremoniously to her new lodging. There the promised servant is waiting for us. She is standing near one of the trees. She is a girl of middling height, aged about fifteen, and not at all ugly. As she had no clothing except a simple leaf which plainly came neither from the Louvre nor from the Bon Marché but perhaps from the Magasin du Printemps as St. Bérain cheerfully suggests, she looks like a fine statue in black marble.

At the moment, the statue is busy gathering something from the trees.

"She's gathering caterpillars; she'll clean them out and dry them and then—don't be surprised!—she'll make them into sauce," explains Dr. Châtonnay, who seems to be well up in negro cookery. "They are called *Cétombo*. They are the only sort fit for eating, and they're said to taste very pleasant."

"That true." Moriliré agrees. "Them good!"

Having seen us, the young negress comes up.

"I," she tells Mlle Mornas, speaking to our great astonishment in almost perfect French, "I was brought up in a French school and I've been servant to a white lady, the wife of an officer. When I returned to my village, I was taken prisoner in a big battle. Know how to make bed like white lady. You quite happy."

While speaking, she gently takes Mlle Mornas by the hand and leads her into the hut.

We turn in, pleased that our comrade is certain of some comfort. But the time for sleep hasn't yet come, either for her or for us.

Indeed, half an hour has scarcely passed when Mlle Mornas again calls us to her help.

We dash over once more, and in the torchlight we see an unexpected sight.

The little black servant is stretched on the ground near the threshold of the hut. Her back is marked, zebra-fashion, with red weals, and the poor child is sobbing fit to break one's heart.

Before her, and protecting her with her body, Mlle Mornas —really superb when she loses her temper—is holding at bay a huge negro who, a few steps away, is making horrible grimaces and who is still grasping a blood-dappled stick. We ask for an explanation.

"Just think of it," Mlle Mornas tells us, "I had hardly gone to bed. Malik—the little negress is called Malik—was fanning me and I was just dropping off. Then here comes this big brute, her master, coming home unexpectedly. As soon as he sees me he flies into a rage, drags the poor child out, and starts beating her unmercifully to teach her to bring white people into his hut!"

"Pleasant manners!" come from the thin lips of the jovial M. Baudrières.

He's quite right, the joval M. Baudrières. But he goes astray when, taking advantage of the position, he puts on an oratorical pose and delivers this surprising statement:

"There you are then, gentlemen, there's these savage tribes whom you hope to turn into peace-loving voters!"

He plainly thinks he's in the Chamber.

M. Barsac starts as though a fly has stung him. He controls himself and answers dryly: "As though Frenchmen never beat their wives!"

He's not far wrong, either, M. Barsac.

Are we about to enjoy a battle of eloquence? No. M. Baudrières not having replied, M. Barsac turns to the negro with the stick.

"The child is leaving you," he tells him. "We're taking her away with us."

But the negro objects. The negress is his slave. He's paid for her. Shall we waste time explaining that slavery has been abolished in French territory? He would never understand. It will take more than a day to reform their customs.

M. Barsac had found a better way. "I'll buy your slave," he says. "How much?"

Bravo, M. Barsac! That's a good idea! Seeing a chance of making a bargain, the negro quietens down. He asks for a donkey, a gun, and fifty francs.

"Fifty blows with a stick," the captain replies. "That's all you deserve!"

They chaffer. At last the rascal parts with his servant for an old flint-lock, a piece of cloth, and twenty-five francs. It's really giving her away.

While the discussion proceeds, Mlle Mornas has lifted Malik to her feet and is dressing her wounds with Karité butter. The bargain made, she leads her to our camp, dresses her in a white blouse, and puts a few coins in her hand.

"Now," she says, "you're not a slave any longer. I set you free."

But Malik bursts into sobs. She says she is alone and she doesn't want to leave "so good a white lady." She will be her chambermaid and will serve her faithfully until she dies. She weeps, she implores.

"Keep her, little girl," St. Bérain puts in. "You'll certainly find her useful. She'll render the thousand little services which a woman always needs—even when she's a man."

Hardly has Mlle Mornas agreed than she must feel like dying of envy. Malik, not knowing how to show her gratitude for St. Bérain's intercession, flings her arms round his neck and kisses him on both cheeks. He tells me next day that he's never known anything more disagreeable. I need hardly add that Mlle Mornas does not wish to experience native hospitality a third time. We pitch a tent for her and nothing else disturbs our sleep.

That's our first day.

The others will no doubt resemble it. So I won't describe them in detail; unless anything else is said, these words will always be understood : *Ab una disce omnes.*[1]

AMÉDÉE FLORENCE.

[1] "As one, so all the others" A quotation from Virgil.—I.O.E.

CHAPTER V

SECOND ARTICLE BY AMÉDÉE FLORENCE

AMÉDÉE FLORENCE'S second article appeared in *L'Éxpansion Française* for the 18th January.

THE BARSAC MISSION
(By despatch from our Special Correspondent)

Daouhériko, 16th December. Since my last despatch written in the midst of the bush on the evening of our departure by the flickering light of a lantern, the journey has been pleasant, and hence it has no history.

The 2nd December we strike camp at five in the morning, and our column, now larger by a unit—or rather should I say by half a unit, for one white is worth two blacks?—gets on the march.

A donkey has been unloaded and its load shared out among the others, so that Malik can have it. Like the child she is, the little negress seems to have forgotten her recent unhappiness. She does nothing but laugh. Happy nature!

Since then we have kept on our route, which is still good and easy. But for the colour of the people and the poverty-stricken countryside, we might think we had never left France.

For the country is not attractive. The district we are crossing is flat, or at least has only slight depressions, with, here and there, some half-hearted hills on the northern horizon. So far as eye can see, we can observe nothing but this stunted vegetation, a mixture of shrubs and grasses two or three yards high commonly called the *bush*.

Here and there is a clump of trees, thinned out by the fires which periodically devastate these savannahs during the dry season. Occasionally we pass some cultivated fields, the *lougans*, as the native word is, usually succeeded by some fairly tall trees. It is then that we approach the villages.

They have absurd names, these villages: Fongoumbi, Manfourou, Kafou, Ouossou, etc. I give it up. Can't they call themselves Neuilly or Levallois like everybody else?

There's no need to say that the leader of the Mission goes into the most miserable villages and holds a palaver with its inhabitants.

Behind him, M. Baudriéres does not fail to make his counter-enquiry.

The two draw, as might be supposed, conclusions diametrically opposed from what they see and hear, so much so that they return equally delighted. So everybody is happy. It's perfect.

For the rest, we are traversing or following the rivers, also with unpronounceable names, and we pass from one valley to another almost without noticing it. That's not of breath-taking interest.

Wherever I look in my notes, I can find nothing worth while confiding to contemporary history until the 6th December. On that date M. de St. Bérain, who is rapidly becoming my friend, fancied that he ought to think up something for my amusement. And, I hope, for yours.

That evening we are camping near a village, a little less insignificant than the others, called Oualia. At the proper time I go into my tent, with the legitimate aim of getting some sleep. There I find St. Bérain, undressed to his vest and pants; his outer garments are thrown about everywhere. The bed is made. At first sight it's clear he means to sleep in my tent. I pause at the entrance to watch what my unexpected guest is doing.

St. Bérain doesn't seem surprised to see me. For that matter, he's never surprised. He is very busy and uneasy, ferreting everywhere, even in my kit-bag, which he has opened and whose contents he has thrown on the ground. But he cannot find what he wants, and that annoys him. He turns towards me, and without seeming at all surprised at seeing me, he says in tones of the utmost conviction:

"I hate absent-minded people. It's disgusting."

I answer without blushing: "Disgusting! But what's happened to you, St. Bérain?"

"Just imagine," he replies, "I can't lay my hand on my pyjamas. I bet that wretch Tchoumouki has left them behind at our last halt. That's cheerful!"

I suggest: "So long as they're not in your own kit-bag?"

"In my...."

"This one belongs to me, my dear fellow, just as this hospitable tent and that virtuous couch belong to me!"

St. Bérain rolls his startled eyes. He suddenly realizes his mistake, hastily picks up his scattered garments and dashes out as if he'd got a horde of cannibals at his heels. I just sink on to my bed and curl up on it.

He's splendid!

Next day, the 7th December, we have just sat at table after our morning march when we see some negroes who seem to be watching us. Captain Marcenay orders two men to go after them. They clear off, only to reappear a little later.

"Chase away the native, and he gallops back," are words thought appropriate by Dr. Châtonnay[1], who has a habit of citing relevant—or more often irrelevant—lines which have usually no relation with the subject. But everyone to his taste.

Moriliré, sent out to investigate, tells us that these blacks, about ten in number, are traders and witch-doctors who have no hostile intentions and simply want to sell us their produce and to entertain us.

"Lock up the silver!" M. Barsac suggests humorously, "and show them into the dining-room!"

So the blacks are shown in, each more ugly and more sordid than the others. Among them are craftsmen, masters of thirty-six trades, makers of pottery, trinkets, baskets, objects in wood or iron; and vendors of weapons, fabrics and especially Kola nuts, of which we lay in an ample store. We realize the

[1] No doubt with reference to the similar proverb about driving away *nature!*—I.O.E.

value of that fruit, which Dr. Châtonnay calls food of thrift, and were very glad to get so much of it in return for a little salt. In the lands we are traversing, salt is scarce; one might almost say, priceless. The further we get from the coast the more valuable it is, so we've brought several bars.

We then summon the witch-doctors and ask them to sing their finest song in honour of our gracious company.

These troubadours from negro-land are two in number. The first holds a guitar. What a guitar! . . . Imagine a calabash crossed lengthwise by three shoots of bamboo each provided with a catgut string. The second witch-doctor, his eyes afflicted by the ophthalmia which is common here, is armed with a sort of flute, a reed with a small calabash fixed at each end.

The concert begins. The second witch-doctor, clad only in a sort of girdle three inches wide passing between his legs, begins to dance, while his companion is more decently covered by a long blouse—of a repulsive dirtiness however—sits down, twangs his guitar, and utters some guttural cries which, I think, are meant to be a song addressed to the sun, to the moon, to the stars, and to Mlle Mornas.

The contortions of the one, the howlings of the other, the strange noises which the two virtuosi draw from their instruments, are sufficient to excite our muleteers. They leave their millet, their rice, and their maize, and organize a ballet which, to put it mildly, is out of the ordinary.

Carried away by their example, we seize the saucepans and cooking-pots, and hammer on them with the spoons and forks; M. de St. Bérain breaks a plate, uses the halves as castanets, and begins a weird sort of fandango with your humble servant as his partner.

M. Barsac—dare I mention this?—M. Barsac himself, throwing aside all restraint, makes a turban out of a towel, and while M. Baudrières, the honourable Deputy from the North, veils his face, the honourable Deputy from the Midi performs a dance of an ultra-meridional abandon.

But all good things must come to an end. After five minutes

of this hullabaloo we have to stop, worn out. Mlle Mornas laughs till she cries.

It's on the evening of this very day that the undersigned, Amédée Florence, gets very indiscreet. To tell the truth, this is a fault I'm prone to, the besetting sin of the journalist.

So, this very evening, chance having placed my tent beside that of Mlle Mornas, I'm just going to lie down when I hear talking next door. Instead of closing my ears, I listen. That's my sin.

Mlle Mornas is talking to her servant, Tongané. He replies in a very weird English, which I translate for my readers' benefit. No doubt the conversation has been going on for some time. She's asking Tongané about his life. As I begin pricking up my ears, she says:

"How did an Ashanti like you. . . ."

Hullo! So Tongané isn't a Bambara! I wouldn't have thought it.

". . . become a Senegalese Tirailleur? You told me once, when I engaged you, but I have forgotten."

Illusion or not, I don't feel she's sincere. Tongané replies. "It was after Captain Blazon. . . ."

Blazon? . . . That name recalls something. But what? Still listening, I rummage among my memories.

"I was taking part in that expedition," Tongané goes on, "when the English came and opened fire on us."

"Do you know why they opened fire?" asks Mlle Mornas.

"Because Captain Blazon had rebelled, and he was robbing and murdering everywhere."

"Is that true?"

"Quite true. They were burning the villages. They were killing the poor negroes, the women, the little children. . . ."

"And was it Captain Blazon who ordered such cruelties?" Mlle Mornas insists; her voice seems different.

"No," replies Tongané. "We never saw him. He never came out of his tent since the other white man came. It was he who gave us orders in the Captain's name."

"Had he been with you long, this other man?"

"Yes, a long time. Perhaps five or six months."

"Where did you meet him?"

"In the bush."

"And Captain Blazon had welcomed him at once?"

"They never parted, until the day when the Captain no longer left his tent."

"And I suppose it was after that day that the cruelties began?"

Tongané hesitates. "I do not know," he declares.

"But that white man," Mlle Mornas asks. "Do you remember his name?"

At that moment a noise outside drowns the voice of Tongané. I don't know his reply. After all, it's nothing to me. Whatever it might be, that story isn't up-to-date, and so it doesn't interest me much.

"What happened after the English opened fire on you?" Mlle Mornas continues.

"I told you that when you engaged me at Dakar," Tongané replies. "I and some of the others, we were frightened, and we escaped into the bush. When I came back nobody was left where they'd been fighting. There were only the dead. I buried several, my own friends, and also the chief, Captain Blazon."

At that point I hear a stifled exclamation.

"After that," Tongané continues, "I wandered from village to village and reached the Niger. At last I came to Timbuctoo, just as the French were entering. It took me over five years to make the journey. At Timbuctoo I joined the Tirailleurs, and when I was discharged I went to Senegal, where you met me."

After a moment's silence, Mlle Mornas goes on: "So Captain Blazon is dead?"

"Yes, missy."

"And you were the one who buried him?"

"Yes, missy."

"Then you know where his grave is?"

Tongané laughs. "Yes indeed," he says. "I could go there with my eyes shut."

Again a silence, then I hear: "Good night, Tongané."

"Good night, missy," the negro replies; he leaves the tent and makes off.

Mlle Mornas turns in, and I'm doing the same without dawdling. But hardly have I put out my lantern when the memory returns.

Blazon? Why the devil didn't I recognize it? Where was my head? What a splendid scoop I missed that day!

I was on the *Diderot* at that time, and—if my personal reminiscence may be forgiven—I had suggested to my chief that I should go and interview the rebel captain on the very scene of his crimes. For months he boggled at the expense. When at last he agreed, it was too late. At Bordeaux, just as I was about to set off, I heard that Captain Blazon was dead.

Now all that is ancient history, and you may ask why I have related this unexpected conversation between Tongané and his "Missy". . . . To tell the truth, I hardly know myself.

On the 8th December, I once more find in my note-book the name of St. Bérain. He is inexhaustible, that St. Bérain. This time it was nothing, but it amused us. Perhaps it may amuse you, too!

We've been travelling two hours in the morning's stage when there's St. Bérain suddenly bursting into inarticulate cries and bouncing about most joyfully on his steed. We are already beginning to laugh sympathetically. But St. Bérain—he does not laugh. He painfully puts his feet on the ground and claps his hand on that part of his anatomy on which he usually sits, meanwhile making inexplicable contortions.

We hurry up to him and enquire: "What's gone wrong?"

"The fish-hooks. . . !" he murmurs mournfully.

The fish-hooks? That doesn't tell us anything. It's only later, when the damage has been repaired, that we understand what he means.

You may not have forgotten that, when, just as we were

leaving Konakry, St. Bérain, recalled by the voice of his aunt —or of his niece—had come hurrying to join us, he had been stuffing a handful of fish-hooks into his pocket. Naturally he hadn't given them another thought. It was the said fish-hooks which were now taking vengeance on his forgetfulness. A careless movement had interposed them between the saddle and the horseman, and three of them had implanted themselves solidly in their owner's flesh.

It takes the intervention of Dr. Châtonnay to free St. Bérain. Three slashes of his scalpel are enough, but the doctor cannot keep from accompanying them with an appropriate commentary. And he laughs as though he were enjoying it!

"Anyone would say you've had a 'bite'!" he remarks as he proceeds to examine the scene of operations.

"Wow!" is the only reply of St. Bérain, who has just been taken off the first hook.

"Good fishing—it's a fine catch!" is the doctor's second remark.

"Wow!" St. Bérain cries anew.

Then, for the third: "You can pride yourself on having made the finest catch of the season," the good doctor compliments him.

"Wow!" St. Bérain sighs for the last time.

The operation's over. It now only remains to bandage the patient, who then remounts his horse, where during the next two days he adopts some remarkable attitudes.

On the 12th December we reach Boronya. This would be a small village like all the others if it hadn't the advantage of owning a particularly amiable chief. This chief, who is quite young, hardly more than seventeen or eighteen years old, makes many gestures, and gives some blows of his whip to his inquisitive people when they try to come too close to us. He rushes up to us, his hand on his heart, and makes a thousand promises of friendship, to which we respond by offering him salt, gunpowder, and two razors. The sight of these treasures makes him dance with joy.

By way of thanking us, he orders a number of straw huts to be built outside the village for us to sleep in. When I take possession of mine, I find the natives very busy flattening the ground and covering it with dried ox-skin. I ask them why the luxury of such a carpet; they reply that it is to keep the white maggots from coming out of the ground. I express pleasure with their attention, and reward them with a handful of cowries. So delighted are they that they at once spit on the walls and rub in the spittle with the palms of their hands. St. Bérain, who is to share my hut—and who is there, for a wonder!—tells me that this is to show me honour. Many thanks!

On the 13th December, in the morning, we reach Timbo without incident. This agglomeration, the most important we have passed so far, is surrounded by a *tata,* a wall of compressed earth, behind which a wooden scaffolding is raised to serve as a sort of circular road.

The *tata* of Timbo really encloses three villages, separated from each other by great stretches of cultivated or wooded land, where the domesticated animals wander freely. In each of the villages there is a small daily market, but in the largest a larger market is held weekly.

One hut in every four is left unoccupied. It is filled with rubbish and miscellaneous filth, as indeed are the streets. The place is certainly short of sweepers. It's not only dirty, it's poverty-stricken. We have seen children, most of them as thin as skeletons, looking for food among the garbage. As for the women, they are repulsively ugly, which, however, does not keep them from being, by all native standards, stylish.

Timbo, as I have explained is the first centre of any importance that we've reached. So we halt there for two days, the 13th and 14th December. Not that we are very tired, but the beasts of burden, and those other beasts, the porters, show a quite understandable weariness.

During these forty-eight hours we've made, one or another of us, a number of excursions within the limits of the *tata,* but don't expect me to give descriptions which you will find quite easily and at great length in the special treatises. My own task is to be historiographer of the Barsac Mission, and that task suits me. Clio inspires me, but I haven't the soul of a geographer. Let this be said once and for all.

The day after our arrival, the 14th, we've been greatly perturbed because of our guide. We searched for him all day, but in vain. Moriliré had disappeared.

But you can be reassured. On the 15th, when we are to set off, he's back at his post, and when we wake up he has already distributed enough blows of his truncheon for the muleteers to have no doubt about his being there. Asked by M. Barsac, Moriliré holds to it that he had never left the camp the day before. As we are in fact not quite certain, and as the matter is not very important, for Moriliré can easily be excused for having wanted to "go ashore" as the sailors say, do not press it, and the incident is closed.

We leave Timbo, then, on 15th December, at the usual hour, and our journey continues all day without special difficulty, and according to the usual time-table. It is to be noted, however, that the hoofs of our horses no longer disturb the soil of the road we've previously followed. That route, beyond Timbo, has little by little become a mere footpath. So now we've really become explorers.

Another change: the country has become more varied. There's nothing but ascents and descents. On leaving Timbo, we have first to climb a fairly lofty hill and then to descend it. The hill is followed by a plain, then comes another hill up to Daouhériko village, beside which we have to stop to camp for the night.

Men and animals being well rested, we travel faster than usual, and when we arrive at the village it's only six in the evening.

The most friendly greetings await us. The chief comes up to us and offers us gifts. M. Barsac thanks him. Cries of welcome respond.

"They didn't welcome me any more warmly when I was at Aix," M. Barsac says with satisfaction. "I knew it. You've only got to talk to them."

He seems to be right, although M. Baudrière shakes his head sceptically.

However, the village headman continues to be amiable. He offers to put us up in the finest huts of the village, and begs our fair comrade to accept the hospitality of his own dwelling. This warm welcome touches our hearts, and the rest of our journey seems rose-coloured until Malik, coming up to Mlle Mornas, says hurriedly and softly:

"You not go, missy! You die!"

Mlle Mornas looks at her in amazement. It goes without saying that I am listening, as is the duty of a self-respecting reporter. But Captain Marcenay is listening also, although it isn't his job. At first he seems surprised. Then, after a short reflection, he decides.

He at once gets rid of the importunitites of the headman and gives orders to make camp. I listen, and conclude that we are well protected.

These precautions make me thoughtful. The captain, who knows negro-land, does he believe in the danger Malik warns us about?

Then?...

Then I must ask myself this question before going to sleep:

"Which is right, M. Barsac or M. Baudrières?"

Perhaps I shall know to-morrow.

In the meantime, I'm perplexed.

AMÉDÉE FLORENCE.

CHAPTER VI

M. AMÉDÉE FLORENCE'S THIRD ARTICLE

THE third article from its special correspondent with the Barsac Mission appeared in *L'Éxpansion Française* on 5th February. For reasons then unexplained, this was the last communication which that journal received from its able reporter.

THE BARSAC MISSION
(From our special correspondent)

Kankan, 24th December. We arrived here yesterday morning and we are setting off early to-morrow, on Christmas Day.

Christmas! . . . My thought flies back to *la patrie,* so far away. (Four hundred miles beyond Konakry). I dream, with a yearning I would never thought possible, of plains covered with snow; and, for the first time for many years, I feel a strong desire to place my feet on the hearth, which would at least prove that I had one.

But we mustn't linger; let us return to the point where we left the proceedings of the Barsac Mission.

As I said in my earlier article, at the moment when the headman of the people of Daouhériko invited us to accept their hospitality, Malik told Mlle Mornas in her own language:

"Don't go there! It will cost you your life!"

That sentence, which the Captain understood, inspired the decision for us to camp outside the village, just where we had halted. Captain Marcenay, after a discussion with Malik, gives orders covering the situation, and tells the natives to clear out. They do not go without protesting their goodwill, but the Captain will not let himself be swayed, and tells them firmly to go to their own quarters and not to come within five hundred yards of our camp. It will soon be seen that these precautions were not in vain.

M. Baudrières, faithful friend of prudence, strongly approves this course, although he does not know its reasons. M. Barsac, on the other hand, who is already seeing himself borne in triumph through laurel arches decorated with tricolour ribbons, cannot conceal his disgust.

No sooner have the natives withdrawn than he comes up to Captain Marcenay, who is standing a couple of paces from me, so that I lose nothing of the scene, and says in a brusque and angry voice: "Who is in charge here, Captain?"

"You, Monsieur le Deputé," replies the officer, coldly but politely.

"Then why, without asking my opinion, have you given orders to camp instead of accepting the inhabitants' hospitality? And why have you driven off these good negroes, who have the kindest intentions towards us?"

With almost a theatrical sense of timing, the Captain waits a moment and then replies calmly:

"Monsieur le Deputé, if, as Chief of the Mission, you are entitled to choose the route and regulate the march as you think best, I too have my duty to perform, which is to protect you. It is true that I should have warned you and told you my reasons, but I wished first to attend to more urgent duties. I ask you to overlook it if I have neglected that...."

So far, so good. Captain Marcenay has expressed regret for his remissness, and M. Barsac could feel satisfied. Unfortunately—possibly a rivalry of a very different kind has had something to do with it—the captain is nervous, although he has been keeping himself under control, and he lets slip a clumsy word which sets fire to the gunpowder.

"If I have neglected that formality," he ends.

"Formality!" repeats M. Barsac, red with anger.

He is from the Midi, M. Barsac, and the folk of the Midi are said to have quicksilver in their veins. I feel that some foolishness is likely.

Trembling with anger, he continues: "And now, at least, will you deign to let me know your motives? They must certainly be strong for you to feel them so much?"

There, I say to myself, there's the rub. It's now the captain's turn to be annoyed. He replies in a dry tone: "I've just heard of a plot against us."

"A plot!" M. Barsac exclaims ironically. "Among these good negroes! At twenty miles from Timbo! . . . Well, really! . . . And who told you about this 'plot'?"

You ought to hear how he pronounces the word "plot". He puffs out his cheeks and rolls his eyes. Heavens, he must think he's back in Marseilles!

The Captain replies laconically, "Malik."

M. Barsac begins to laugh. And what a laugh!

"Malik! That little slave that I bought for a handful of sous!"

He exaggerates. First of all, Malik is not a slave, seeing that there's not a slave in French territory. A Deputy ought to know that. And then, Malik was quite expensive. It was as much as twenty-five francs that she cost, plus an old gun and a piece of cloth.

None the less he continues: "For a few sous! There's a fine authority, indeed, and I agree you ought to have been frightened."

The captain feels the blow. At the word "frightened" he makes a face. He controls himself, but you can feel that he's boiling over with fury.

"You will allow me not to share your alarm," M. Barsac goes on, however, he too is getting more and more annoyed. "I am going to be a hero! So I'm going to the village to sleep, and I'll conquer that robber's lair all by myself."

I can foresee all sorts of foolishness. But I am forestalled.

"I am not advising you," replies the captain, giving tit for tat. "I don't know if Malik is, or is not, mistaken, but as it's doubtful I must take the course which prudence demands. I repeat that I am responsible for your safety. My instructions on this point are formal, and I shall not neglect them—if need be, in spite of you."

"In spite of me!"

"So if you try to infringe the orders of the military commandant and leave the camp, I shall regretfully have to place you under guard in your tent. And now I am at your service, Monsieur le Deputé. I have to see to the camps being set up, and I have no leisure to argue further. I have the honour to wish you good night."

With that, the captain raises his hand to his *képi*, executes a right turn in regimental style and goes off, leaving the Deputy from the Midi in a state bordering upon apoplexy.

To tell the truth I didn't wander far myself.

M. Barsac's annoyance is the greater because the scene has taken place in Mlle Mornas' presence. He is about to follow the captain, plainly meaning to pick a quarrel which might end badly, when our amiable companion checks him with a word:

"Stay with us, Monsieur Barsac. The captain was wrong, certainly, not to have told you, but he has apologized, and you have hurt him yourself. After all, in protecting you in spite of yourself he's only doing his duty, at the risk of making you angry and hindering his own advancement. If you are at all generous you will thank him."

"That's too much!"

"Now calm down, please, and do listen to me. I've just been talking to Malik. It was she who warned M. Marcenay about the plot which is being hatched against us. Have you ever heard of the *doung-kono?*"

M. Barsac shakes his head. He is no longer fuming, though he's still making faces.

"I know about it," comes an interruption from Dr. Châtonnay, who had just joined us. "It's a deadly poison, and it has the strange effect of not killing its victims until eight days later. Do you know how they prepare it? It's very queer."

M. Barsac does not seem to be listening. The extinct volcano is still smoking.

Mlle Mornas replies for him: "No, Doctor."

"I will try to explain," says Dr. Châtonnay, not without a certain hesitation, "although it's rather a delicate matter. . . . Oh well! Let's get on with it! You must know then, that, to make the *doung-kono,* they take a stalk of millet and introduce it into the bowels of a corpse. Three weeks later they take it out and dry and crush it. They put the powder into milk, or sauce, or wine, or some other drink, and, being tasteless, it gets swallowed without being noticed. Eight to ten days later begins the swelling. The abdomen especially swells up in an incredible style. After forty-eight hours death ensues, and nothing, no antidote, no remedy, can save you from:

> ". . . *ce destin funeste, qui*
> *S'il n'est digne d'Atrée, est digne de Thyeste*"[1]

Good! Another quotation! I can see that it rhymes, certainly, but what's the point?

"And now," says Mlle Mornas, "this is the plot the villagers are hatching. When she got here, Malik heard the headman of Daouhériko talking with the other chiefs of the district. Dolo Sarron—that's the name of this petty prince—was going to receive us amiably and to invite some of us into his home, and the others into his accomplices' huts. There they were going to give us food or some local drink, and we should not have refused it. Meanwhile they would also have given drink to the soldiers. . . . To-morrow we should set off without noticing anything, and in a few days we should begin to feel the first effects of the poison.

"Of course every negro in the region would be waiting for that moment; and, once our convoy was disorganized, they would steal our goods, enslave our muleteers and porters, and

---

[1] This quotation, which comes from an eighteenth-century tragedy—a real blood-curdling thriller—by Crébillon, was also used by Poe at the end of his short story *The Purloined Letter*—I.O.E.

seize our horses and donkeys. Malik discovered the plot and warned Captain Marcenay, and you know the rest."

You can well imagine how we received that news. M. Barsac is struck with consternation.

"There! What did I tell you?" says M. Baudrières triumphantly. "There you are, there's your civilized peoples! These dirty scoundrels!"

"I can't believe it," groans M. Barsac. "I'm bowled over, literally bowled over! This Dolo Sarron, with his friendly manner! Oh! But we'll have the last laugh! To-morrow I'll burn down the village and as to this wretch Dolo Sarron...."

"Don't think of it, Monsieur Barsac," cries Mlle Mornas. "Remember that we have hundreds and hundreds of miles to cover! Prudence...."

M. Baudrières interrupts her. He asks: "Do we really have to push on with this journey? The question was put to us: 'These people in the Niger Bend—are they, or are they not, civilized enough to have political power bestowed on them?' I think we know the answer. Our experience during the last few days, and especially this evening, ought to be enough!"

Thus assailed, M. Barsac starts to reply. He draws himself up. He's going to make a speech. Mlle Mornas forestalls him.

"M. Baudrières is too sweeping," she says. "Like the Englishman who insisted that all the French are red-haired because he met someone of this colour when he landed at Calais, he's judging a whole people by a few exceptions. As though crimes were never committed in Europe!"

M. Barsac agrees forcibly. But his tongue is itching. He bursts into speech.

"Quite right!" he exclaims. "But, gentlemen, there is another side to the question. Is it conceivable that the representatives of the Republic, hardly on the threshold of a mighty enterprise, will allow themselves...."

He speaks well, does M. Barsac.

"... will allow themselves to be discouraged at the outset like frightened children? No, gentlemen, those who have the honour of bearing the French Flag should have a firm common sense and a courage which nothing can quell. But they will fully realize the gravity of the risks which they are to run, and these dangers fully known, they will face them without blenching. But these pioneers of civilization. . . ."

Heavens, it's a speech! And what a time to make it!

"These pioneers of civilization must, above all, use circumspection and not be too ready to make sweeping statements about a vast country by simply basing it on one sole fact whose very accuracy is uncertain. As the previous speaker put it so admirably. . . ."

The previous speaker was simply Mlle Mornas. She smiles, does this previous speaker, and to cut short this flow of eloquence, she starts applauding loudly. We follow her example—except for M. Baudrières, that goes without saying.

"Then that's settled," says Mlle Mornas in the midst of the din, "and the journey goes on. I repeat then that prudence demands that we avoid any bloodshed, which might involve reprisals. If we are wise, we will make it our first aim to go on peaceably. At least, that's Captain Marcenay's opinion."

"Oh, well, if that's Captain Marcenay's opinion!" M. Barsac agrees, half convinced, half doubtful.

"Don't be sarcastic, Monsieur Barsac," replies Mlle Mornas. "You would do better to go and find the captain, whom you certainly snubbed just now, and offer him your hand. We may, indeed, owe him our lives."

M. Barsac is hot-headed, but he's a good fellow and a good man. He hesitates a little before making such a sacrifice, then goes off to Captain Marcenay, who has just finished posting the camp guard.

"Just a word, Captain," he says.

"At your command, Monsieur le Deputé," responds the captain, adopting a military attitude.

"Captain," M. Barsac continues. "We were both wrong just now, but myself more than you. I ask you to forgive me. Will you do me the honour of giving me your hand?"

I can assure you that these words are said with much dignity and have nothing humiliating about them. Captain Marcenay is quite moved.

"Ah, Monsieur le Deputé," he says. "It is too much! I have already forgotten it."

They shake hands, and I feel that, until something else turns up, they will be the best friends in the world.

The Barsac-Marcenay incident having been closed to the general satisfaction, we all go off to the shelter provided for us. I am about to turn in when I see that, after his usual custom, M. de St. Bérain isn't there. Has he gone out of camp, then, in spite of the orders?

Without telling my companions, I set out to look for him. I suddenly chance upon his servant, Tongané, who says: "You wish see massa Agènor? You come softly. See him hiding. Him very funny!"

Tongané leads me to the edge of a tiny stream inside the line of sentinels, and there, hidden behind a baobab, I see St. Bérain. He seems very busy and his fingers are holding some animal which I cannot see clearly.

"Him got *ntori*," Tongané tells me.

A *ntori* is a toad.

St. Bérain pulls open the jaws of the brute and thrusts into its body a steel rod sharpened at both ends. To the middle of this rod a string is attached, and he's holding the other end.

The queer thing is that during the whole of this operation St. Bérain never stops giving heart-rending sighs. He seems to be suffering cruelly, and I cannot imagine why. But I have hit on the key to the riddle. Though he's suffering, it's only because of the barbarous way he's treating the unlucky *ntori*. Even when he yields to his passion for fishing, his gentle nature rebels.

After placing the toad in the grass along the bank, he crouches down behind a tree, a thick stick in his hand, and waits. We do likewise.

We do not have to wait long. Almost at once a weird-looking animal appears, a sort of huge lizard.

"You see," Tongané says quietly. "There good *gueule-tapée*."

"Big mouth?" The doctor told me yesterday that this means a sort of iguana.

The big-mouth swallows the toad, then tries to get back into the water. Feeling itself trapped by the cord, it struggles, and the steel points stick into its flesh. It's caught. St. Bérain pulls the creature towards him, and raises his stick.

But what's up? The stick falls slowly while St. Bérain gives vent to a groan. . . . Once, twice, thrice, the stick rises menacingly; once, twice, thrice, it falls inoffensively, to the accompaniment of a lamentable sigh.

Tongané loses patience. He bounds out of our hiding-place and he's the one who, with a vigorous blow, puts an end to the hesitation of his master and to the life of the big-mouth, which has never so much deserved its name.

St. Bérain gives another sigh, this time of satisfaction. Already Tongané has picked up the iguana.

"Morrow," he says, "we eat *gueule-tapée*. Me make cook. Him very good."

It was indeed "very good."

On the 16th December we set out at dawn. We go round the village and can see only a few of its people about at so early an hour. That old rascal Dolo Sarron watches us file past, and I think he's menacing us with a gesture.

A little before nine, the footpath is broken by a river, as usual swarming with hippopotami and crocodiles. We have to look out as we cross it. I notice that this is the first time we've to do so. Until now, either we've found bridges or else the water's been so low that our mounts had scarcely got their hooves wet. This time it's different: before us we really have a river.

Fortunately its level is lower than we feared. Our horses go in only up to their flanks and we cross without any difficulty.

But for the donkeys it's another matter. When these animals, already fully loaded, are brought to the river bank, they halt with one accord. In vain the muleteers try to urge them on. They show as little response to cries of encouragement as they do to blows.

"Oh, I know," says one of the muleteers. "Them want baptised!"

"Yes, yes!" replies his colleagues. "Them want baptised."

Each of them then lifts a little water and pours it over the animals' heads, pronouncing some unintelligible words.

"That's an immemorial custom in these parts," M. Tassin explains. "At the first ford they have to cross, the rule is to baptise the donkeys. You'll see that as soon as the ceremony is carried out they'll go on without any trouble."

And in fact before long they do.

It's then about 86° in the shade. The donkeys, probably finding the coolness of the water pleasant, no doubt feel that a good bath would be more enjoyable still. After two or three joyous brays, they gaily tumble over in the river and roll about with so much delight that their insecure loads start drifting away.

They have to be fished out. The muleteers set to work with their typical sagacious slowness, so that, but for Captain Marcenay's soldiers, we should have lost half our provisions, our presents, and our trade goods, and that would have been irreparable bad luck.

While M. Barsac is breathing out his impatience and his ill-temper in violent language and hurling Provençal epithets at the slow-moving muleteers, Moriliré goes up to him:

"*Mani Tigui* (commander)," he says sweetly. "You no shout."

"Not get into a temper! . . . When those beasts want to drown my goods to tune of a hundred thousand francs!"

"Not good," answered the guide. "You, much patience. If burdens fall, natives argue, you no shout. Then talk much, but no wicked. Later, all be much good."

What I am writing here, exact though it is, may not amuse you much. If so, there's nothing I can do about it. When setting off to follow the Barsac Mission, I expected some thrilling reportage, and I hoped to send you some copy teeming with fabulous adventures. Mysterious shadows in the virgin forests, struggles against nature, combats with wild animals, battles with armies of countless negroes—that was what filled my dreams. I must disillusion myself. Our forests, they're simply the bush, and we haven't encountered any natural obstacles. As regards animals, all we have seen have been hippopotami and crocodiles, plenty of them certainly. To these we must add herds of antelopes and, here and there, a few elephants. As for negroes thirsting for blood, all we've met have been friends, except for that old brigand of a Dolo Sarron. The journey is quite monotonous.

After leaving Daouhériko of unhappy memory, we have first to climb a hill, then we redescend to Bagareya, in the Tinkisso valley. I now notice, for lack of anything more exciting, that Tchoumouki has left the rear-guard and is walking alongside Moriliré. Has he had a row, then, with Tongané? Tchoumouki and Moriliré are chatting together and seem to be the best friends in the world. Come along! So much the better!

As for Tongané, he doesn't seem to be missing his comrade much. In the rear of the convoy he's entertaining himself with little Malik, and the conversation seems quite animated. An idyll, perhaps?

Beyond Bagareya we are again in the bush, which is becoming increasingly arid in proportion as we get further from the rainy season, and once more we are on the plain, which we did not leave until we reached Kankan to-day.

During the 22nd, at Kouroussa we cross the Djoliba, which M. Tassin assures me is the Niger; but at Kankan we find another river no less great flowing towards the first, which it joins, apparently, thirty miles towards the north. Why shouldn't it be that this river, which they call the Milo, that is the veritable and authentic Niger? M. Tassin, not without a somewhat scornful look, assures me that it isn't, but he doesn't tell me why. I don't care, either way.

And adventures, you ask me. What, in nine days, has nothing happened?

Nothing at all, or very little!

In vain I scan my note-book with a magnifying-glass. I can find only two facts at all worthy of being mentioned. The first is trifling. As for the other! Ah! Well! The other, I don't know what to think about it.

Here is a brief account of the first.

Three days after we left Daouhériko, we were making our way without effort between *lougans* fairly well cultivated, a sign that we were nearing a village, when three natives crossing our path suddenly showed clear signs of fear and took to their heels.

"*Marfa! Marfa!*" they cried, while making the best use of their legs.

Marfa means "gun" in the Bambara language. But we didn't at all understand the meaning of this exclamation: so as not to frighten the negroes, Captain Marcenay had decided that his men should hide their weapons in raw-hide sheaths not at all suggestive of their nature. So there weren't any rifles visible. So why the terror of the negroes as they crossed our path?

We were vainly asking ourselves, when we heard a metallic clatter, followed by a cry of indignation from St. Bérain.

"The rascals," he howled furiously. "They're throwing stones at my angler's case! Look at it, all dented! Wait, just wait a bit, you wretches!"

We had all the trouble in the world to keep him from chasing the attackers, and at last Mlle Mornas had to intervene. The negroes, seeing his fine nickel case glittering in the sun, had taken it for a rifle barrel. Hence their fright.

To avoid any similar misunderstandings which might have landed us in some awkwardness, M. Barsac begged M. de St. Bérain to place this over-brilliant article on the donkey's back

among the luggage. But there was no way of making this
obstinate fisherman see reason; he declared that nothing in the
world would make him put away his lines. All we could get
was that he should wrap up his nickel case in a piece of cloth,
so as to hide its brightness.

He's a character, my friend St. Bérain.

The other happening took place at Kankan, where we
arrived twelve hours later than we expected, on the morning
of the 23rd, simply because Moriliré had been missing again.
On the 22nd, just as we were getting *en route* for the second
stage of our journey, no Moriliré. We hunted for him on all
sides in vain, so we had to resign ourselves to wait.

Next morning, very early, our guide was again at his post,
and getting ready to set off as though nothing had happened.
This time he couldn't deny his absence. He explained that he
had had to go back to the last camp, where he had left Captain Marcenay's maps. The captain berated him soundly and
the incident was closed.

I would not have even mentioned this if St. Bérain, in his
usual style, hadn't tried to make it seem more important by
misrepresenting it.

Being unable to sleep that night, he had, it seemed, been
up when our guide returned. Then he went on to say, very
mysteriously, that it was not to Captain Marcenay that
Moriliré returned, nor from the west whence we ourselves
had come, but from the east—from towards Kankan where
we were going; and so he could not have been looking for
something he had forgotten, and that, in fact, he had been
lying.

Coming from any other source, such news would deserve
consideration, but coming from St. Bérain! St. Bérain is so
absent-minded he would not know north from south.

Getting back to business, I told you that the other incident
took place at Kankan. While we were strolling, Mlle Mornas,
M. Barsac, St. Bérain and I, under the guidance of Tchoumouki and Moriliré. . . .

But I see that I've forgotten to make myself clear, so I'd better start a little further back.

Understand then that, for several days, Moriliré has never stopped pestering us, one after another, by singing the praises of a certain medicine-man; to be more precise a *Kéniélala* (fortune-teller) living at Kankan. According to him, this *Kéniélala* possesses an astonishing "second sight," and time and again he pressed us to test him personally. I need hardly say that with one accord, and without consulting one another, we sent him about his business. We hadn't come into the heart of Africa to consult clairvoyants, however extra-lucid they may be.

But, while we are walking around Kankan under their guidance, here come Moriliré and Tchoumouki stopping a few steps from a hut which at first sight looks not at all out of the ordinary. By chance, which I suspect them to have abetted, we seem to be exactly before the residence of the famous *Kéniélala* they've been praising so highly. Once again they advise us to visit him. Once again we refuse. But they won't take no for an answer, and again they imperturbably begin to sing the praises of the venerable witch-doctor.

What's it got to do with Moriliré or his friend Tchoumouki if we visit their *Kéniélala?* Have the customs of this land advanced so much that the two rascals will get a "commission" on the proceeds of their phenomenon, and are they expected to bring clients to him, as the gondoliers of Venice bring them to the glass-work and lace manufacturers? There's something that M. Barsac would approve of.

The two compères are not discouraged. They insist so much that we give way, if only to have some peace. After all, we can give them a little pleasure, and if it brings them a few cowries, so much the better for them.

We enter a hut, abominably dirty, penetrated by only a gleam of light. The *Kéniélala* is standing in the middle of the room. After having slapped himself for five minutes on the thigh while saying *Ini-tili*, which means "good midday",—for that is the time—he squats down on a mat and invites us to do the same.

He begins by piling up in front of him a heap of very fine sand, which he spreads out fan-wise by one movement of a little broom. Then he asks us for a dozen Kola nuts, half red and half white, which he moves rapidly over the sand while babbling incomprehensible words; then, setting them out on the sand in several figures, circles, squares, diamonds, rectangles, triangles, and so forth, he makes strange gestures above them as though he were blessing them. At last he collects them carefully and holds out his dirty hand, in which we place the consultation fee.

Now we've only got to ask him. He is inspired. He speaks.

In turn we ask several questions, while he listens in silence. He will give all the answers at once, he tells us. When we have finished, it's his turn to speak, very volubly and very quickly, like a man who is certain of what he says. Not very cheerful, the predictions of our magician! If we had any faith in him—which fortunately we haven't—we should come out of his consulting-room worried and ill at ease.

He starts with me, with me who's been enquiring about the fate of what I value most in the world, the articles I'm sending you.

"Soon," he tells me in a gibberish which I am translating into decent French, "nobody will have any more news of you."

So that's my fortune! Still, the witch-doctor has said "Soon." So I can be at ease about the present letter.

The *Kéniélala* passes on to St. Bérain.

"You will get," he foretells, "a wound which will keep you from sitting down."

I think about the fish-hooks. He's a bit late, the old humbug. His mind's wandering in the past, on the shadows of which Moriliré and Tchoumouki have doubtless not failed to cast a light.

It's Mlle Mornas' turn now:

"It's in the heart that you will be wounded," the *Kéniélala* declares.

Oho! Not so stupid! Observe that he hasn't been very precise. Will the wound be physical or moral? As for me, I lean towards the second hypothesis, and I have a shrewd suspicion that our two guides have passed on a little "gossip." Mlle Mornas must have interpreted the prophecy as I have, for she's blushing. I'll wager she's thinking about Captain Marcenay.

But our magician has become silent, and now looks at M. Barsac with an air of menace. Clearly we are about to hear the most important of the predictions. He prophecies:

"Beyond Sikasso, I can see white men. It is slavery or death for you all."

He's a cheerful fellow, the old grandfather.

"White men?" repeats Mlle Mornas. "You mean black."

"I have said: 'white men'," comes the solemn declaration of the *Kéniélala,* who is feigning inspiration most amusingly. "Do not go beyond Sikasso. Beyond, slavery or death."

Needless to say, we took the warning lightly. Who does this story-teller think is going to believe that on French territory there's a band of white men so numerous that they can threaten a column as strong as ours?

At dinner that evening, we laugh over the story, even the nervous M. Baudrières, and then we think no more about it.

But I think about it again this evening when I turn in. I think about it very seriously, and at last I come to some conclusions which . . . that. . . . But you can judge for yourself.

Let us first set out the problem.

There are two facts and a half.

The half fact is the absence of Moriliré at Timbo, and then at our last halt, before Kankan.

The two facts are the attempted poisoning by the *doungkono* and the sinister prediction of the black magician.

That being clear, let us consider.

First fact. Is it credible that the chief of a paltry village would have thought up a crazy scheme for attacking a Mission guarded by two hundred sabres, and that in a region long occupied by our troops, only twenty-five miles from Timbo, an important post garrisoned by the French? No, it is unbelievable. Indeed, it is inadmissible, absolutely inadmissible.

Second fact. Is it conceivable that a stupid and ignorant old negro has the power of reading the future? No, he hasn't got any such power, that's certain.

But the *doung-kono* incident is just as certain—at least I feel that though such a scheme could not have been seriously considered, it has been specially faked to make us believe it's authentic.

Similarly, it is certain that the *Kéniélala*, who left to himself would have spoken at random and told us something quite different, has not in fact done this, but has insisted in predicting slavery or death for us beyond Sikasso.

The conclusion is inescapable : someone is trying to frighten us.

Who? Why? I ask you.

Who? I haven't the slightest idea.

Why? With the aim of making us give up our journey. We are becoming a nuisance to somebody, and that somebody doesn't want us to go beyond Sikasso.

As to the half-fact about Moriliré, either that doesn't mean anything, or, if St. Bérain was not so absent-minded as usual, Moriliré is an accomplice of those people who are trying to stop us. His insistence on taking up to the *Kéniélala* already makes him suspect, and it is credible that he has at least been hired for that purpose. This point will have to be cleared up.

Such are my conclusions. The future will show whether they are, or are not, well founded.

Qui vivra, verra.

AMÉDÉE FLORENCE

In the bush, a day's march from Kankan, 26th December.

I add a postscript to yesterday's letter, which Tchoumouki has undertaken to send off to you.

What happened last night is extraordinary. I tell you about it without even trying to explain it.

We left Kankan yesterday morning, and, after two long stages of about twenty miles all told, we camped last night in the open. This region is sparsely inhabited. The last village we passed, Diangana, is about twelve miles behind us, and it is thirty miles to the next, Sikoro.

At the usual hour, the camp turns in.

In the middle of the night we are suddenly aroused by a strange noise, which none of us can explain plausibly. It is a loud roaring, resembling that of a steam-engine, or, to be more precise, like the buzzing of insects, but of gigantic insects, of insects the size of elephants.

According to the sentries' reports, this unexpected noise began towards the west. At first very weak, it gradually grew louder. By the time we've come out of our tents it is at its highest. The queerest thing is that it comes to us from above, from the air, from the sky. Whatever causes it must be almost overhead. But what can this be?

In vain we strain our eyes. Impossible to see anything. Thick clouds hide the moon, and the night is as black as ink.

While we are vainly trying to pierce the darkness, the roaring goes towards the east, fades, dies away. . . . But before it has quite gone, we hear it again approaching us from the west. Like the first, this roaring increases, reaches its maximum, fades and ceases, going off towards the east.

The camp seems terror-stricken. All the negroes are hiding their faces in the ground. The Europeans have grouped themselves around Captain Marcenay. Among them I can see Tchoumouki and Tongané who, by dint of living among white people, had gained something of their firm spirit. On the other hand, I cannot find Moriliré. No doubt he is lying flat on his stomach somewhere with those of his own colour.

Five times the terrifying roaring begins, increases, and dies away. Then the night resumes its usual calm and ends without further disturbance.

In the morning it's quite a business to get the column to form up. The natives are scared and absolutely refuse to budge. Captain Marcenay at last brings them to reason. He shows them the sun, rising in a cloudless sky. Certainly nothing out of the way is now happening in the air.

At last we set off, three hours late.

The events of the night naturally form the subject of all our conversation, but nobody can explain them. Little by little, however, we start talking about other things. Then, a mile and a half beyond our camp, Captain Marcenay, who is going on ahead, notices that the earth is grooved by some ruts about four inches deep at the western end, petering gradually towards the east. There are ten of them in five groups of two.

Have they got anything to do with the events of the night? One is at first tempted to answer : No.

And yet there is the direction common to them all from west to east and their numbers are similar : five groups of ruts, five successive roarings.

Well?

Well, I don't know.

AMÉDÉE FLORENCE

CHAPTER VII

AT SIKASSO

On the 12th January, the Barsac Mission had arrived at Sikasso, about 700 miles from the coast.

Though *L'Éxpansion Française* was not receiving further articles from Amédée Florence, that able reporter was still keeping his note-book up-to-date, and it is from this that the following narrative is taken.

To judge from his records, the journey from Kankan to Sikasso was monotonous and devoid of interest. A few jokes were made about St. Bérain, and his absent-mindedness, and there were the ordinary incidents of travel, none of them worth quoting. Tchoumouki seemed to be avoiding his old comrade Tongané and was becoming increasingly friendly with the leading guide, Moriliré, but nobody took any notice of that.

None of the dismal forebodings of the *Kéniélala* showed any signs of being fulfilled. Amédée Florence went on writing his articles and giving them to Tchoumouki, who always promised to send them off; and if for some reason or other they did not arrive, the reporter knew nothing of that. Bérain could still bestride his horse. The heart of Jane Mornas had received no wound, or at least no visible wound—though in a figurative sense, this prophecy seemed more likely to be fulfilled than the others, as Florence recorded in a few sympathetic lines.

As regards the fourth prediction, the most serious and the most sinister, nothing, absolutely nothing, suggested that it was ever likely to be justified. The Mission was neither destroyed nor reduced to slavery; it was advancing peaceably under the protection of Captain Marcenay's two hundred sabres; its animals were in good health and not more of its luggage had been lost in crossing the rivers than was to be expected with negroes.

AT SIKASSO

Moreover, the conclusions which Amédée Florence reached at the end of his third article had not been confirmed. Nobody had risked making an attack on the column, and no other *Kéniélala* had been met with to utter his dismal forebodings. So if the reporter had been right, and somebody had cherished the absurd plan of scaring the Mission into retiring, he seemed to have abandoned it.

Indeed, Florence himself did not feel too certain about this plan. The facts on which his opinion was based gradually lost their cogency as they faded into the past. Although the expedition had not reached Sikasso, beyond which the danger was supposed to arise, he felt more reassured every day, so absurd did it seem that the inoffensive negroes whom they met should risk attacking a large body of regular soldiers.

He might, however, have felt a little less certain about basing his peace of mind on the escort had he remembered that soon it was to be halved.

For it was at Sikasso that the Mission was to divide. While the first half, led by Barsac in person, was to push on to the Niger and return by way of Dahomey, the second, under the guidance of Baudrières, would turn southwards towards Grand-Bassam. Obviously both halves of the Mission would have an equal right to protection, so that the escort would have to be reduced to a hundred men for each.

Sikasso itself was a mere group of villages separated by cultivated fields and enclosed by the usual *tata;* within this the French administration had constructed the buildings needed to house the troops which formed its garrison.

This then consisted of one company of Colonial Infantry and two of Senegal Tirailleurs, these led by French officers and N.C.O's. The delight of these young fellows, so long separated from their comrades, may well be imagined when they saw the arrival of the Barsac Mission. It rose to its height when they recognized the commander of the escort, for Captain Marcenay found several old friends in this distant outpost. It became almost delirious when they realized that the expedition included a white girl.

The new arrivals were honoured by a ceremonial welcome. Flags waving in the breeze, bugles sounding, drums beating, triumphal arches wreathed in foliage, applauding negroes picturesquely grouped together—nothing was lacking, not even an address by Barsac.

That evening the officers entertained their new friends at a magnificent party remarkable for its sparkling gaiety. Jane Mornas presided, with a success which need not be dwelt on. Everybody surrounded her, even thronged around her, for all these ardent young officers would gladly have fought for a smile from this girl who had brought a ray of sunshine into their exile.

But the head of Jane Mornas was not turned by popularity. Among all the compliments she received, those of which Captain Marcenay was not sparing found the quickest way to her heart. This preference she showed so unconsciously, so innocently, that it was realized at once. So Captain Marcenay's comrades, like true Frenchmen, were considerate enough to limit their enthusiasm, and in turn they showered on the fortunate officer discreet compliments which he in vain disclaimed deserving.

Marcenay tried to avoid their gaze, denied everything, swore that he did not know what they meant. Yet he understood them well enough, and wallowed in his happiness. So it seemed that his day-dreams were to be realized—Jane Mornas' feelings were so obvious that he had been the only one not to recognise them! In this way the two first realized their affection for one another.

Next day began a discussion about the manner in which the Mission was to be divided, and this quickly led to unforeseen difficulties.

For the Europeans, nothing could be easier. Around Baudrières were grouped MM. Heyrieux and Quirieu, conformably to their instructions, and M. Tassin, conformably to his own wishes. To Barsac were joined M. Poncin and Dr. Châtonnay. Amédée Florence also opted for that party, as its route was longer and so likely to give him more copy.

Captain Marcenay's orders were to detach a hundred of his men, commanded by a lieutenant from the garrison, as escort for Baudrières. He himself, along with the other hundred, was to remain with Barsac. Compelled to comply strictly with these instructions, he was greatly perturbed: which of the parties would be chosen by Jane Mornas?

What a sigh of relief he gave on hearing that, when consulted on the subject, she announced that she would go with Barsac! But how different was his sigh of disillusionment this time, following close upon the first, when she added that she and St. Bérain meant to remain only a few days with the honourable deputy from the Midi; after a few marches she intended to leave the party to continue her own exploration further north.

There rose from the officers a general cry of indignation; one and all regarded her as most unwise for considering so risky a project. What, alone, without an escort, she wanted to risk herself in regions almost completely unknown, where French arms had not yet entered? They explained that such a journey was impossible, that she would be risking her life, or at least that the village headmen would oppose her movements.

This achieved nothing. Jane Mornas remained inflexible, and nobody, not even Captain Marcenay, had the slightest influence upon her.

"You're wasting time," she said laughingly. "The most you will do is to scare my uncle—look at him rolling his great frightened eyes!"

"Me!" protested Agénor, thus drawn into the dispute.

"Yes, you," Jane Mornas insisted. "You're half dead with fright, that's easy to see. Are you going to be influenced by these birds of ill omen?"

"Me!" repeated poor St. Bérain.

"What are you afraid of?" asked Jane superbly. "I shall be with you, my dear nephew."

"But I'm not afraid!" St. Bérain protested, enraged at being the cynosure of all eyes.

Jane Mornas turned her back on his denials.

"No," she said, "I left Europe with the idea of traversing the Hombori and reaching the Niger at the top of its Bend, at Gao. I shall traverse the Hombori and I shall reach the Niger at Gao."

"And what about the Touareg Aouelimmiden, who occupy both banks of the Niger in that district?"

"I don't give a fig for the Touareg," replied Jane Mornas, "and I shall go on in spite of them."

"But why Gao rather than anywhere else? Why do you have to go there? After all, you're travelling for pleasure."

"I want to," Jane Mornas replied.

The officers agreed that this was quite a good reason and very French, and they all admired her pluck.

"It's a splendid motive," Commandant Vergèze decided. "When a lady wants anything, that settles it and we're not going to be the ones to argue."

The division of the higher personnel being settled, all that remained to be done was to make a fair division of the rank and file—that seemed quite easy.

First of all, the ten donkeys, the five muleteers, and the ten porters really belonging to Jane Mornas and St. Bérain naturally followed the fate of their employers. The other porters and muleteers and the rest of the animals were divided into two unequal groups, the larger being allocated to the Mission which was to make the longest journey, that of Barsac, to whom was also assigned the guide Moriliré. Agreement was reached without difficulty on such points.

But it was when it was sought to put these arrangements into effect that the trouble began.

When first spoken to on the subject, Moriliré categorically refused, and no argument could bring him to reason. He declared that he had been engaged only to go as far as Sikasso, and that nothing in the world would make him go further. In vain every argument was used, and even intimidation: all that he would consent to do was to accompany Baudrières southwards. When it came to going eastwards with Barsac, it was impossible to move him.

That point having been conceded after some trouble, similar difficulties arose regarding the muleteers and the porters. Except for those directly engaged by Jane Mornas and her nephew, they unanimously refused to go beyond Sikasso. Entreaties, promises, threats, all were in vain. The expedition was up against a stone wall, and had to give up trying to convince them.

So a search had to be made for a fresh guide as well as fresh servants. There was no great difficulty in securing the latter, but several days elapsed before the expedition at last found a native guide in whom they felt enough confidence.

At once Moriliré underwent a sudden change of heart. He, who had listened with complete indifference, even it seemed a little disdainfully, to the fruitless entreaties of his superiors, had suddenly changed his attitude the moment their efforts were crowned with success. He sought out Barsac, humbly begged pardon for his obstinacy, which he said had been due to fright, and offered to lead the Mission on to Dahomey, as he had been engaged to do. At the same time, all resistance vanished among the former porters and muleteers, who declared themselves ready to follow their guide wherever he wished to lead them—but on the sole condition that this guide would be Moriliré.

This sudden unanimity clearly showed that the said Moriliré was alone to be held responsible for that unexpected strike, and it was felt for a moment that his tardy offer should be declined. But as it was desirable to be certain of the assistance of an experienced personnel, and of a guide born in the district, it was finally decided to turn a blind eye to his conduct.

Thus the new guide would be assigned to Baudrières, with a small group of the former personnel, and several of the new porters. Barsac would keep Moriliré and most of the original porters and muleteers.

All these hesitations, all these changes, had taken some time. Though they had arrived together at Sikasso on the 12th January, it was not until the 21st that Barsac and Baudrières could leave it separately.

That morning, at dawn, once more the companies were under arms and drawn up on parade under their officers, once more the flags fluttered in the breeze, once more the bugles sounded, and the Barsac Mission, followed by the Baudrières Mission, defiled between a double line of soldiers. Then the troops, moving off behind them, escorted them as far as the edge of the enclosure.

Beyond the *tata* there was an exchange of farewells. The officers of the garrison wished them a pleasant journey; and, not without some emotion, Barsac and Baudrières shook hands. At last, as the troops returned to their barracks, the two convoys set off and put themselves *en route*, each in its own direction.

Baudrières, his companions, and the hundred men of their escort went off towards the south. Barsac, M. Poncin, Dr. Châtonnay, Amédée Florence, Jane Mornas and St. Bérain, similarly escorted by a hundred horsemen commanded by Captain Marcenay, turned to the left and disappeared towards the east.

These two columns, so very similar, were to have very different destinies. If the first was not to encounter any real danger, or even any serious difficulty, it was not so for the second. While Baudrières went on to accomplish his mission peaceably, and to assemble the material for his report to the Chamber, and at last arrived at Grand-Bassam almost on schedule, Barsac and his friends were to be involved in the most terrible, the most extraordinary, adventure that could be imagined.

So ignoring the petty incidents which marked the quiet progress of Baudrières, this narrative will henceforth deal exclusively with that part of the Mission which set off eastwards, and which, led by the guide Moriliré, plunged ever more deeply into darkest Africa.

CHAPTER VIII

MORILIRÉ

(*From the note-book of Amédée Florence*)

22nd January. It is now two days since we left Sikasso, and already I have an idea that there's something wrong. It is only an idea, I repeat, but I feel that the spirit of our servants has fallen off; our muleteers are showing less ardour, if that were possible, in hurrying on the donkeys, and our porters are tiring more quickly and demanding more rests. Maybe this is all imagination, and I am unconsciously influenced by the predictions of the *Kéniélala* at Kankan. Though I had almost forgotten them, they seem to have regained a certain cogency since now that we have left Sikasso our escort has been cut by half.

Do I feel anxious? Not at all! Oh rather, if I am uneasy it is lest that idiot of a *Kéniélala*, instead of merely pattering off his lesson by rote, actually has second-sight. What is it I really want? Adventures, adventures, and still more adventures from which I can get good copy, because that's my job. But adventures, real adventures, are what I'm still waiting for.

23rd January. I can't help thinking that we are going along like a convoy of tortoises. Certainly the nature of the ground doesn't lend itself to rapid progress; it's nothing but going up and coming down. None the less, the ill-will of our negroes seems unmistakable.

24th January. What did I tell you? This evening we reached Kaféle. We have taken four days to cover about thirty miles. Eight miles a day, that isn't bad—as a record.

31st January. Well, we've beaten our record! We've taken six days to do another thirty miles or so—total, sixty miles in ten days!—and here we are in a little place called Kokoro. What a hole!

Three days ago we left a village called Ngaga—where the devil do they hunt up these names?—we've climbed another of those steep hills, then made a steep descent into the valley we're now following. Mountains to the north, south, and west. Before us, eastwards, the plain.

To add to our bad luck, we were delayed some time in Kokoro. Not that we were prisoners. On the contrary, the village headman, a certain Pintié-Ba, is our very good friend.

At Kokoro begins the country of the Bobos. If the name is rather amusing, the inhabitants are less so. Mere brutes.

For one thing, these rascals are not fussy about food. They'll eat without repugnance what is nothing but decaying carrion. Pah! And their mentality is comparable, as can be seen from the way we came into contact with them.

The scene is Kokoro, yesterday, 30th January. It is night. Just as we reach the village we are jostled by a howling mob of negroes—we could count in the torchlight at least eight hundred—who do not seem to be inspired by the most friendly intentions. It's the first time we've had a reception of this kind. So we halt, rather taken aback.

Taken aback, but not alarmed. Let those lascars brandish their weapons as they will, we know we could wipe out those charming folk with a single volley. Captain Marcenay gives an order. His men grasp their rifles, but don't take them out of their cases. Indeed, the captain hesitates. To fire on a neighbour is a serious matter, even when that neighbour is a Bobo. So far our powder has been silent, and we don't want to make it speak.

That is the position when St. Bérain's horse, frightened by the din, pulls up suddenly with his four feet apart. Shot out of the saddle, St. Bérain makes a graceful somersault and falls slap into the horde of negroes.

They start howling wildly, and are throwing themselves upon our unlucky friend when. . . .

. . . when Mlle Mornas spurs her horse into their midst. This at once draws their attention from St. Bérain. They surge round his courageous squire. Twenty assagais are levelled against her.

"*Manto!*" she cried to her assailants. "*Nté a bé souba*" ("Silence! I'm a witch!")

As she says this, she takes a pocket electric torch from her saddle-bow and switches it on and off, to show plainly that she can control fire and the lightning.

At sight of this, the howling ceases and a great circle forms respectfully around her; to the middle of this comes Pintié-Ba, whom I've already mentioned. Of course he has to make a speech. That's the weakness of every government on earth. But Mlle Mornas silences him. First she has to go to the help of St. Bérain, who has not moved since his fall and might have been injured.

This is soon verified by Dr. Châtonnay, who enters the circle as calmly as though it were the home of one of his patients: St. Bérain is wounded. He is indeed covered with blood. He fell so unluckily that a pointed stone cut deeply into him just below the loins.

I saw at once that this fulfils one of the *Kéniélala's* predictions. It has come true. That gives me such good hopes for the others that it sends a shiver through me whenever I think of the fate of my articles.

However, Dr. Châtonnay has cleaned up the wound. He takes out his instrument-case and sews up the injury, while the negroes look on in amazement.

While this operation is proceeding, Mlle Mornas, who has stayed on her horse, gives Pintié-Ba permission to speak. He approaches and wants to know, in Bambara or some such gibberish, why the *toubab* (meaning St. Bérain) had attacked them with a gun. Mlle Mornas denies it. The headman insists and points to the case which St. Bérain is carrying like a bandolier. She explains. Labour lost. To convince him, the case, which shines in the torch-light, has to be uncovered and opened, and the fishing lines it contains have to be displayed.

At the sight, the eyes of Pintié-Ba gleam with envy. His

hands extend towards that shining object. Like a spoiled child, he wants to have it, he must have it, he insists. St. Bérain indignantly refuses.

Mlle Mornas, who wants to consolidate the newly-formed peace, presses him in vain. At last she gets angry.

"Nephew!" she says severely, while shining her torch-beam towards the recalcitrant angler.

St. Bérain at once yields up his case to Pintié-Ba, who attributes his success to the magic power of the electric torch and the influence of the witch.

When the idiot has got hold of his treasure, he goes wild with joy. He dances the devil of a jig; then, at his signal, all the weapons vanish and he advances into our midst.

He treats us to a discourse in which he invites us, it seems, to wander around the village just as we please, and he orders that the following day there shall be a grand dance in our honour.

In view of the peaceful attitude of the Bobos, Captain Marcenay sees nothing inconvenient in our accepting the invitation. The following day, therefore—that's to-day—early in the afternoon, we pay our visit to our new friends, while our escort and our black personnel wait outside the *tata*.

Ah, dear readers, what a performance! Tastes differ, but so far as I'm concerned, I prefer the Champs-Elysées.

We go straight to the palace. This is an agglomeration of huts in the midst of the village, near the central pile of garbage—which isn't meant to make them smell pleasant. On the outsides these huts, built of compressed earth, are daubed with ash. But it's their insides you ought to see! The yard is nothing but a mud-patch serving as a meadow for the cattle and sheep. All around are the dwellings, which are more like cellars, for you have to go downwards to get into them. Don't try it! You smell an abominable stink which takes you by the throat, and you have to fight your way through the goats and hens and other farmyard animals which stroll about so freely.

From this description of the palace you can well imagine what the dwellings of the common herd are like. They are dens of swarming rats, lizards, millipedes, and other vermin, in the midst of all manner of filth, from which comes a disgusting stench.

A charming place!

It is in the palace that the official reception takes place. It consists of giving Pintié-Ba some presents, otherwise useless, from a few pieces of cloth to padlocks without keys, and from old flint-lock pistols to some needles and thread.

Literally dazzled by these splendid presents, he gives the signal for the dance.

First the musicians go through the village, some playing the *bodoto*, a trumpet made of antelope horn, others the *bouron*, a different kind of trumpet made of elephant tusk, still others on the *tabala*—in English, the drum. Two men carry the *tabala*, on which a third beats with all his might, using a sort of club, called the *Tabala Kalama*. Regarding this, Captain Binger has pointed out, quite reasonably, that *Kalama* sounds if it were derived from *Calamus*, so that *Tabala Kalama* literally means a pen to write on the drum.

At the sound of this medley of instruments, the Bobos gather on the market-place, and the feast begins.

A sort of Soudanese Punch, the *mokho misai kou*, enters and dances with remarkable grimaces and contortions. He is clad in a red robe and capped with a bonnet adorned with cows' tails, from which a piece of cloth falls to cover his face. He carries, bandolier-fashion, a bag filled with clanking lumps of iron, and each of his movements jangles little bells and rattles fastened to his ankles and wrists. He cheerfully tickles the faces of the audience with long cow-tails.

When he has finished these exercises, which seem to give much amusement to Pintié-Ba and his courtiers, the latter, on a sign from their leader, roar like wild beasts; this, I suppose, means unanimous applause.

Silence restored, Pintié-Ba sends for an umbrella adorned

with cowries and amulets, not because he needs it but because a headman is nothing unless he has, wide opened above his head, the parasol, the emblem of power.

Then the dances begin. Men, women, children, form a circle, the witch-doctors bang on the drums, and two female dancers run in from the opposite ends of the place. After three rapid pirouettes, they run up to one another, not face to face but on the contrary turning their backs on each other, and, when in contact, bumping each other as hard as possible.

To these two danseuses follow two others, and at last all the audience, howling savagely, joins in a sort of disordered quadrille, compared with which our wildest dance would seem very modest and very dull.

The dance ends with a procession. The Bobos file past Pintié-Ba, singing a chorus to the accompaniment of the deafening noise of the *tabala*, the trumpets, and the cane flutes, whose strident sounds rend the ears.

At last it is supper-time and then begins a scene of carnage, an orgy of blood.

They bring in a dozen or so sheep, killed in the huts. They stretch long cords from tree to tree; this marks out a square, in which the women pile up some dry wood. Then with their knives the negroes hack the animals into pieces and cut them into strips which the women hang on to the cords, while the wood is kindled. When he thinks they are properly cooked, Pintié-Ba gives a signal, and all the negroes rush headlong on the strips of meat, grip them by the handful and tear them with their teeth. They find nothing too repulsive. It is a horrible sight.

"They are cannibals!" cries Mlle Mornas. She has turned quite pale.

"Alas, yes, dear child," Dr. Châtonnay replies. "But if eating is the only pleasure these unfortunate people have, it is because they are always suffering from the same complaint— hunger."

Disgusted, we make no delay in going back to our tents,

but for the negroes the feast goes on late. It indeed lasts all night, as is shown by the outcries which reach our ears.

2nd February. We are still at Kokoro, delayed by St. Bérain's injury. The uncle-nephew (I at last call him this) cannot stay on his horse.

3rd February. Still Kokoro. That's cheerful!

4th February, six a.m. At last we're off!

The same day, evening. False start. We are still at Kokoro.

This morning, at dawn, we made our farewells to our friends the Bobos. (One has friends where he can find them). All the village is standing, Pintié-Ba at their head, and there comes a litany of greetings. "May *N'yalla* (God) keep you in good health!" "May He give you a good road!" "May He give you a good horse!" at the sound of this last wish St. Bérain makes a face—his wound is still painful.

We tear ourselves away from these demonstrations, and the column gets off.

It gets off, but it does not get on. It's worse than it was before Kokoro. The ill-will is glaringly evident. Every moment a porter stops and we have to wait for him. A donkey's load tumbles off and we have to put it on again. At ten, when we halt, we haven't gone four miles.

I marvel at Captain Marcenay's patience. Never once has he swerved from the most perfect calm. Nothing upsets him, nothing tires him. He struggles with a quiet cold energy against this campaign of obstructiveness.

But, when we set out for the evening's march, it is another matter. Moriliré declares that he has made a mistake. We consult the two guides hired by Mlle Mornas.

Tchoumouki agrees with Moriliré. Tongané declares on the other hand that we are on the right road. That's very helpful! What are we to believe?

After long hesitation, we accept the majority opinion, and return on our tracks. Then it's marvellous to see how fast we go. The blacks are no longer tired, the donkey-loads have secured themselves.

In an hour we have covered the distance which took four going the other way, and, before nightfall, we have regained our morning's camp, near Kokoro.

6th February. Yesterday, 5th February, we set off again without too many difficulties, and what is remarkable, by the very road which we had rejected the previous day. Moriliré now swears, indeed, on thinking it over, that last evening he had been mistaken. Again Tchoumouki supports him. I am strongly inclined to think that these two darkies are in league against us.

Nothing special yesterday, except the ill-feeling we are beginning to get accustomed to; but two grave incidents to-day.

During the morning's march, a donkey falls suddenly. They try to get him up. He's dead. Of course, his death could be natural. I admit, however, that I fancy it might be the *doungkono* or some other filth he has picked up.

Nobody says a word. We simply share the dead beast's load among the others, and continue on our way.

When we move off again in the afternoon, the second incident occurs. We realize that one of the porters is missing. What's become of him? It's a mystery. Captain Marcenay chews his moustache; I can see he's anxious. If the negroes forsake us, we are done for. Nothing is more catching than the germ of desertion. Moreover, I can see that our precautions have now become more stringent. We have to march in file as though on parade, and the horsemen of the escort do not permit the slightest free movement. I find this strict discipline a nuisance, but I approve of it all the same.

When we halt for the evening, another surprise. We see that several of the negroes are drunk. But who has given them the booze?

The captain organizes a most meticulous watch over the camp, then he goes to find M. Barsac, whom I happen to be with at the time, and explains the situation, which has been getting worse since we left Sikasso. Dr. Châtonnay, M. Poncin,

Mlle Mornas, then St. Bérain, come one by one to join us, so that we can hold a regular council of war.

The captain sets out the facts in a few words, and puts the blame on to Moriliré. He suggests giving the faithless guide a thorough questioning, and then if necessary to use force. Each of the negroes should be individually accompanied with a Tirailleur, who will force him to march, even if that means under pain of death.

M. Barsac is not of that opinion, and St. Bèrain even less. To interrogate Moriliré will be to warn him, to show him that he's been found out. We haven't any evidence against him, and what's more we cannot so much as imagine whyever he should betray us. Moriliré has only got to deny it, and we shall have nothing to say.

As for the natives, how can we possibly compel them? What's to be done if they lie down, if they resist us only with the force of inertia? Shooting them would be a very poor means of making sure of their services!

We decide that it would be better to keep silence, to be firmer, to protect ourselves by indomitable patience, and above all to keep a careful watch on Moriliré.

This is all very well, but a thought occurs to me. Why push on so stubbornly with this journey? The object of the Mission is to inform itself of the mentality of the negroes in the Niger Bend and of their degree of civilization. Well, we understand their mentality well enough. If the peoples between the coast and Kankan, indeed so far as Tiola or even Sikasso, are said to be rough-hewn enough to deserve some political rights, I'll willingly agree, although that's not my own opinion. But beyond Sikasso? . . . It won't be these savages all around us, these Bobos who are more like animals than men, who are to be converted into voters, I suppose? Then why be so determined? Isn't it clear that the further East we go, which means the further from the sea, the less contact the natives have had with Europeans, and so their veneer of civilization (?) will wear thinner and thinner.

These truths seem dazzlingly clear to me, and I am amazed that my travelling companions don't find them equally dazzling.

All things considered, perhaps they are dazzled, but they may have their own reasons for closing their eyes to them. Let's look into this.

Primo: Captain Marcenay. For him the question does not arise. The captain is not there to argue but to obey. Moreover, I cannot imagine that even without orders he would so much as think of retiring, so long as Mlle Mornas goes forward. The sympathy they feel for one another has shown much more progress since we left Sikasso than that of ourselves. We have before us an official attachment, openly declared on both sides, which should logically end in a marriage—so openly indeed that M. Barsac has spontaneously given up his hopes of making a conquest and has become simply the excellent man he really is. So let's pass on.

Secundo: M. Poncin. He also is a subordinate, and he also obeys. As to what he really thinks in his heart, that remains to be seen. He takes notes from morning to night, but he's so silent he could give points to Hermes himself. I could swear that since we started he hasn't said ten words. My opinion is that he scorns them. So let's leave M. Poncin.

Tertio: St. Bérain. That's quite another matter. St. Bérain sees only through the eyes of his aunt-niece; he lives only for her. And he's so absent-minded he may not even know he's in Africa. So let's pass on from number three.

Quarto: Mlle Mornas. We know quite well why she's travelling. She's told us: because she wants to. That reason is enough, even if we weren't too tactful to wonder whether there's really something else.

Quinto: Myself. This number five is the only one whose conduct is perfectly logical. What's my reason for existing? Copy. So the more difficulties there are the more copy I shall get, and the happier I shall be. So it's quite clear that I don't dream of going back. So I don't dream of it.

There remains M. Barsac. He owes obedience to nobody, he is not in love with anybody, he cannot help realizing that we are in Africa, he is too serious-minded to give way to a whim, and he hasn't any copy to place. So? . . .

This question worries me so much I'm going to ask him outright.

M. Barsac looks me up and down, nods his head, and makes a gesture that doesn't mean a thing. That's all I can get out of him. Anyone can see he's used to being interviewed.

7th February. Things have been happening, and the night has been disturbed. Result: we didn't get off at the usual hour, and to-day we shall make only one march, in the evening.

Let's set down the facts in chronological order. The conclusion that may be clearly drawn from them is that upsets can sometimes be useful.

We had decided yesterday to say nothing to Moriliré and to limit ourselves to watching him more closely. With that purpose, and so as to keep him under our eyes without letting the rank and file of our escort into the secret of our fears, we have to keep watch in turn. As there are six of us, including Mlle Mornas, who always regards herself as a man, that won't be too much of a business.

To keep to that programme, we have divided the night, from nine to five, into six parts more or less equal, and drawn lots for them. We come out of the hat in the following order: Mlle Mornas, M. Barsac, Captain Marcenay, myself, St. Bérain, and M. Poncin. So fate has decided.

At one in the morning my turn comes, and I take Captain Marcenay's place. He tells me that everything is in order, and he points to Moriliré, who is asleep not far from us, wrapped up in some white garment.

The moon, now at its full, lets us see the fellow's black face and brings the white garment into relief.

Nothing out of the way during my turn of duty, except that, about half past one, I think I can hear the same roaring which had so much bewildered us near Kankan. The noise seems to come from the east, but now it is so distant, so weak, so elusive, that even at the time I was not too sure of hearing it.

At a quarter past two I hand over duty to St. Bérain and turn in. I cannot sleep. Because things are unusual, no doubt, sleep will not return after being interrupted. After half an hour's effort, I give it up, and I get out of bed, with the idea of finishing the night in the open air.

At that moment I again hear—so weakly that I think it might be another illusion—the same roaring noise that recently drew my attention. This time I'm going to make certain. I dash out and stretch my ear towards the night.

Nothing, or rather, so very little! A sound like breathing which fades, fades and dies very gradually towards the east. I shall have to resign myself to remaining uncertain.

I decide to go and find St. Bérain, who is just carrying out his tour of duty.

Surprise!—(Indeed! Is it a surprise?)—St. Bérain is not at his post. I bet the hopeless scatterbrain has forgotten his duty and is busy with something else. So long as Moriliré has not taken the opportunity of leaving us without ceremony!

I make certain. No, Moriliré has not absconded. He's still there, sleeping peacefully, stretched on the earth. I can see his black face and his white covering brilliantly lit up by the moon.

Reassured, I set out after St. Bérain, with the idea of giving him a good talking-to. I can pretty well guess where to find him, for I noticed a river flowing not far from our camp. I go straight there, and just as I had expected I can see a shadow in the middle of the current. How did this fanatic of a fisherman manage to get so far from the bank? Can he walk on water?

As he explained this morning, St. Bérain has improvised a raft, just big enough to carry him, out of three lengths of wood; then, using a long branch instead of a punting-pole, he's pushed himself some way out into the stream. There he's moored himself, using a large stone as an anchor, tied to the raft by a fibre cord. Making this took only about half an hour's work. It's quite ingenious.

But at the moment that's not what I'm concerned with.

I go up to the bank and call him softly: St. Bérain? . . ."

The shadow on the water replies "Here!"

I continue: "What are you doing there, St. Bérain?"

I hear a quiet laugh, then the shadow replies: "I'm poaching, my dear fellow."

I must be dreaming! Poaching? . . . In the Sudan? . . . I did not know that fishing rights were preserved here! I repeat:

"You're poaching? What sort of game are you playing?"

"That's right," St. Bérain replies. "I'm fishing by night with a casting-net. It's absolutely illegal."

That idea amuses him. He laughs, the fool.

"And Moriliré?" I ask, exasperated.

There comes through the darkness a terrible oath, which my pen refuses to write, then the shadow begins to move, and St. Bérain, wet up to his knees, comes scrambling on to the bank like a thief. Now he's half-crazy with fright. He's left it a bit late.

"Moriliré!" he repeats in a choking voice.

"Yes, Moriliré, I tell you. What have you done with him, idiot?"

There comes another oath, and St. Bérain makes off for the post he should never have left.

Fortunately Moriliré is still asleep. I could even swear that he hasn't moved since I relieved Captain Marcenay. St. Bérain confirms this.

"You've given me a fright!" he sighs.

At that moment we hear a loudish noise from the river bank we've just left. Anyone would think it was somebody drowning.

We run, St. Bérain and I, and indeed we can make out, on

the far side of his improvised raft, some black object thrashing about.

"That's a negro," says St. Bérain.

He jumps on his raft, disentangles the negro and brings him to the bank, meanwhile explaining to me :

"The rascal has got caught up in my net—I'd forgotten it." (Naturally, my dear St. Bérain). "But what the devil was he doing there?"

We bend over the poor devil, who at last is breathing strongly enough for us not to worry about his fate, and the same cry escapes from our lips :

"Moriliré!"

It is indeed Moriliré, Moriliré completely naked, drenched from head to foot, and half-suffocated by his ducking. It is plain that the guide left the camp, swam across the river, and went for a little walk in the country; then when he came back he got caught up in the net providentially forgotten by St. Bérain. Without our precious scatterbrain, the traitor's absence would have gone completely unnoticed.

Then suddenly a thought flashes into my head : what about the other Moriliré, sleeping so soundly in the moonlight?

I run to that obstinate sleeper, I shake him. . . . Well, I ought to have guessed it; his garment is empty and comes away in my hand. As for the black face, it is only a lump of wood capped by the helmet and plume with which the former Tirailleur embellishes his natural beauty.

This time the wretch has been caught in the act. He'll be lucky if he can explain it.

I go back to St. Bérain and his prisoner, who seems to be painfully returning to life.

I say "seems", for suddenly he makes an artful leap out of our hands and dashes off for the river bank, plainly meaning to have another bath.

Moriliré has reckoned without his host. St. Bérain's hand falls on the wrist of the fugitive, who vainly struggles to escape.

Honestly I think St. Bérain less captivating than the Apollo Belvedere, but he's as strong as Hercules. He must have a terrible grip, if I may judge by the contortions and grimaces of the negro. In less than a minute Moriliré is overcome; he falls on his knees and begs for mercy.

At the same time something drops from his nerveless grasp.

I stoop down and pick up the object. Unfortunately we weren't sufficiently wary of the negro. Moriliré frees himself by a desperate effort, throws himself upon me and grasps the said object in his free hand; it disappears into his mouth.

A third oath from St. Bérain. I go for the captive's throat, while my companion grips his other arm.

Half choking, Moriliré has to give up. But alas, he only gives up by half. With his steel-like teeth, the negro has cut the suspicious object in two, and one half has been engulfed in the depths of his stomach.

I look at my quarry. It is a small piece of paper, with some writing on it.

"Look after that scum," I warn St. Bérain.

St. Bérain reassures me with a word, and I hurry to find Captain Marcenay. His first care is to deposit Moriliré, suitably bound, in a tent, round which he sets four men to whom he gives the most explicit instructions. After that we all go to the captain, clamouring to know what there is on the sheet of paper.

By the light of a lantern, we ascertain that it bears some Arabic characters. The captain, well versed in Arabic, would have no difficulty in reading them, if they were clearer and if the document were intact.

But the writing is very poor, and as I explained we have only half of the text. In its present state it's only a riddle, which the poor light of the lantern does not allow us to decipher. We must wait for daylight.

But when the day comes we reflect that we must be taking a lot of unnecessary trouble. Everything suggests that Moriliré, no longer having any hope of deceiving us, will value our goodwill so much that he will confess his misdeeds and give us the complete translation of the document.

We go up to the tent which forms his prison, and go in.

Amazed, we pause upon the threshold : the cords which held the prisoner are lying on the ground. The tent is empty.

CHAPTER IX

BY SUPERIOR ORDERS

(From the notebook of Amédée Florence)

The same day. I have just had to break off, as Captain Marcenay was calling me to see the translation of the fragment of paper which escaped Moriliré's appetite. I now resume my chronological record.

There we are, finding the tent empty. No trace of Moriliré. Nothing but the rope on the ground. Greatly annoyed, Captain Marcenay questions the guard. But the poor devils are as taken aback as we are. They swear that they have never left their post, and that they heard nothing suspicious. We can't make it out.

We go back into the tent, and then we see for the first time a hole cut into its roof: above this we observe a thick treebranch. That explains everything. Insecurely fastened, Moriliré has somehow or other loosened his bonds, shinned up the tent-pole, and got away, so to speak, by air.

Should we go after him? What's the use? He's got almost an hour's start, and how could we find him in the bush? We should need dogs.

Agreed on this, we yield to the inevitable. The Captain takes down the tent which had held Moriliré so insecurely, dismisses the four Tirailleurs, and orders them on pain of severe punishment not to say a word about what they've seen. Then he goes off to his quarters to attack the mysterious document. Meanwhile St. Bérain will tell our companions all about it—if he doesn't forget it himself.

An hour later Captain Marcenay sends for me, as I've already mentioned. I find him in M. Barsac's tent, where all the Europeans are assembled. Their faces show a natural astonishment. Where's the rhyme or reason in Moriliré's treachery? Is he acting on behalf of some third party, whose

BY SUPERIOR ORDERS

intervention I've long been suspecting? Perhaps we shall know in a few minutes.

"The Arab writing," Marcenay explains, "goes from right to left, but as the paper is transparent we've only to turn it round to read it in the usual way. Here's the result."

He gives us a piece of paper, irregularly torn across, like the original; on this I read, copied in the Latin alphabet, the following words :

> Mansa a man gnigné toubabou
> Memou nimbé mando kafa
> batakè manaèta sofa
> A okato. Batou
> i a ka folo. Mansa a bè

If it were left to me to decipher these cabalistics !

We pass the paper from hand to hand. Mlle Mornas and St. Bérain do seem able to make something of it. I marvel at the extent of their knowledge. As for MM. Barsac and Poncin, they know just as much as I do.

"The last words of the first two lines are incomplete," Captain Marcenay explains. "The first ought to be *toubaboulengo*, which means 'Europeans', literally 'Red Europeans', and the last *Kafama*, meaning '*still*'.

"With these additions, here's the translation of the document : 'The Master (or The King) doesn't want the Europeans. . . . As they are still coming on . . . letter will fetch the soldiers . . . . He will give the orders. Obey . . . you have begun. The Master (or The King) is. . . .' "

We make faces. That's not much clearer.

"The first part is easy to understand." Captain Marcenay continues. "Somewhere there is a 'Master' or a 'King' who doesn't want us to do so and so. For some reason or other he finds us a nuisance. The missing half no doubt begins by describing some plot which we don't know about. The next two lines aren't so clear. 'A letter will fetch the soldiers,' that doesn't tell us much. The fourth is only an order to Moriliré, and we don't know who that 'he' is who will 'give the orders.' As for the last words, they don't mean anything, to us at any rate."

We look at each other disappointedly. That takes us a long way! M. Barsac sums things up:

"From what's happened so far, along with to-day's happenings, we can conclude: *Primo:* our guide has betrayed us for the benefit of some third party who, for some reason unknown, wants to obstruct our movements. *Secundo:* this unknown person must have some influence, for even at Konakry he managed to plant on us a guide whom he had chosen. *Tertio:* this power is not too great, all the same, for so far he's only found childish methods of attaining his ends!"

I raise an objection: "Pardon! the mysterious unknown has made some attempts of quite a different character."

And I explain to my honourable audience my pondering over the *doung-kono* poison and the *Kéniélala's* predictions. They praise my perspicuity.

"These ingenious deductions that M. Florence has made," adds M. Barsac, "all they do is to confirm my own. I say then that our adversary, whoever he may be, need not be feared too much, or the methods he used against us would be far more serious and far more effective."

M. Barsac is right. It is wisdom, Sophia, the great Sophia of the Greeks, that speaks through his mouth. He goes on: "My opinion is this, then, that while giving this business our serious attention, we must take care not to exaggerate it. This comes to saying, let's be prudent, but don't let's worry about it too much."

We all agree, which does not surprise me, for I know the secret motives of all of them. What does surprise me, however, is M. Barsac's obstinacy. Why doesn't he take advantage of this chance of interrupting a journey whose uselessness can no longer be doubted?

Whatever happens, we've got to get some fresh guides. Mlle

Mornas suggests her own; they know, or they ought to know, the country, as that was the very reason she engaged them. To settle the matter, we sent for Tchoumouki and Tongané.

The attitude of the former does not please me. He tells us that we can rely on him, but he seems uneasy and embarrassed, and while he speaks I can never catch his furtive eye. To my mind this fellow is oozing with lies. In my opinion he's no better than Moriliré.

Tongané, on the other hand, is straightforward. He declares that he knows the way quite well, and that he will lead us wherever we want to go. He tells us, too, that he can get the porters and muleteers to see reason. This boy makes a good impression. His tones are candid and he looks you in the face.

I decide that from now on I shall have confidence in Tongané and distrust Tchoumouki.

The two new guides go to hold a palaver with the native personnel. Keeping to the official version, they tell them that Moriliré has been eaten by a crocodile and that henceforth they will take command in his place. Nobody says anything. After the midday rest, we set off.

9th February. Moriliré is no longer here, but it's just the same. With Tchoumouki and Tongané we hardly advance any quicker than with their predecessor.

The two guides keep arguing about the direction we ought to take. They never agree, and their quarrels are endless. I always opt for Tongané's directions, and experience shows that I am right. If the majority happen to decide in favour of Tchoumouki, at the first village we come to we invariably find we are wrong. Then we have to swerve, sometimes across ground which is almost impracticable, so as to regain the good road we'd left.

At other times, the discussions of our two Africans last until the heat of the day comes and we have to stay where we are.

In such conditions, we do not get on very fast. So in two days and a half we've scarcely covered twenty miles. That's poor.

We are still following the valley along which we entered Kokoro. It keeps broadening, and we no longer have any hills southwards, on the right.

The road is one of the easiest, and as there are none of these endless river-crossings, sometimes over wooden bridges three parts broken down, but more often by fords not always very fordable and in which the crocodiles are not at all rare, we have no material difficulty to contend with.

11th February. Early this morning, we came into the midst of cultivated fields, showing that a village is near. These fields would be fairly well kept up were not so much of them devastated by termites, which are terribly destructive.

These insects build mushroom-shaped termitaries, sometimes the height of a man, and at the beginning of winter they leave them like winged ants. Then they infest the villages. But the people never lose a chance of amusing themselves. The appearance of these winged ants is the signal for feasts and nameless orgies. Fires are lighted, and on these the ants singe their wings. The women and children collect them and fry them in Cé butter. Then it's not enough to eat, the people must drink. So, when evening comes, the whole village is drunk.

Towards eight o'clock, we see something that tells us of this village. It is called Bama. Just as we are nearing it, we meet a procession of *dou,* traversing the *lougans* to drive away the evil spirits and pray for rain. These *dou* are dressed in blouses adorned with sprigs of flax and palm-fibre. Their heads are completely covered by flax bonnets with two holes for the eyes and surmounted by a crest in red wood or by the beak of a bird of prey.

They dance along, followed by loafers and boys whom they're never tired of beating with their sacred rods. Whenever they pass a hut, they gulp *dolo* (millet beer) or palm wine. That's as much as saying that after an hour of their promenade they are dead drunk.

Half an hour later, we arrive at Bama. With an hypocritical

air, Tchoumouki tells Captain Marcenay that the natives are over-tired, that they refuse to make another march, and that they want to stay at Bama all day. The Captain is not taken aback and, in spite of the warning signs which Tongané keeps making behind his comrade's back, he looks surprised and says that the request is needless, as he's already decided to make a long halt to-day. Tchoumouki goes away embarrassed, while Tongané lifts his arms to Heaven and expresses his indignation to Malik.

We take advantage of this unexpected halt to visit the village. This interests us, as it's so different from those we've seen so far.

To enter it we have first to get on the roof of a hut, and they take us from roof to roof, as far as that of the headman.

This headman is an old negro with a flourishing moustache and looks like a former N.C.O. of the Tirailleurs. He smokes a long copper pipe, kept alight by an ugly little piccaninny.

He welcomes us very cordially, and offers us some *dolo*. Not to be outdone in politeness, we make him a few small gifts which overwhelm him with joy; then, these ceremonies performed, we stroll around like tourists.

In the square a travelling barber is working in the open air. Near him some boys, pedicures and manicures, aided by a pair of old scissors, gnaw at the finger and toe nails. Four cowries from each client, that's the charge for their services, but they have to hand over the nail-parings to their clients, who make haste to bury them piously in little holes. I enquire vainly, through St. Bérain, who can make himself a little understood; we cannot learn the reason for this strange custom.[1]

A few paces away a 'doctor' is treating a patient according to the prescriptions of the negro Codex. We look on from afar at the 'consultation.'

---

[1] Evidently Florence had not read *The Golden Bough*, which explains that the intention is to keep the parings from being used to "cast a spell" on their owner!—I.O.E.

The invalid is emaciated, his eyes hollow and trembling with fever. The doctor makes him lie on the ground in the midst of a circle of onlookers; then, having bleached his face with moistened ash because in this country white is "magic," he places beside him a little statuette in roughly-sculptured wood, the image of some benevolent god. Then, while emitting savage yells, he performs a grotesque dance round the patient. Then, having had the seat of the illness pointed out, he massages it gently; then suddenly, with a howl of joy, he pretends to pull out a fragment of bone which he has palmed in readiness. The invalid at once gets up and goes away, proclaiming that he is cured, a new proof of the truth of the aphorism that it is only faith that heals.

Wasn't that of our invalid strong enough? There's reason to suppose so, for the benefit he announced doesn't last long. That very evening our camp receives a visit from him. Having learned, from one or other of our negroes that a *toubab* physician was with us, he comes to ask the help of the white witch-doctor, because his black colleague hadn't succeeded in curing him.

After a short examination, Dr. Châtonnay simply gives him a dose of quinine. The patient does not stint his thanks, but as he goes off he shakes his head sceptically, like a man who doesn't think much of a remedy whose strength isn't reinforced by a magic incantation.

12th February. To-day is "same thing" as yesterday, as the men of our escort say. It's even worse. We've so far made only one march, and we shan't do better to-morrow.

This morning we set out in good order.

Just as our column was getting under way, we see yesterday's patient running up to us. He is so much better that he wants to thank his benefactor once again. The doctor gives him a few packets of quinine, with advice on how to use them.

All goes well throughout the march. The pace is lively. Not a hindrance, not a complaint from the negroes. It's too good.

At the hour for the halt, indeed, just as we're settling down,

Tchoumouki comes up to Captain Marcenay and holds a discourse like yesterday's. The Captain replies that Tchoumouki is certainly right, that we shall not start again that night nor all to-morrow, but that then, after so long a rest, we shall not halt for the evening until we've covered at least twelve miles.

The Captain says this loudly, so that nobody can misunderstand him. The negroes realize that in future things are going to be different. But the firm tones of the Captain seem to have impressed them. They say nothing and turn their backs on us while exchanging surreptitious glances.

Same day, eleven at night. This narrative is beginning to bore me.

This evening, about six, and this in broad daylight, we suddenly hear the same roaring noise which had first struck our ears near Kankan and then my own ear-drums on the night of the Moriliré incident.

To-day, as before, this strange noise comes from the east. It is very faint, but loud enough for us not to mistake it. Moreover, I'm not the only one to hear it. The whole camp gazes skywards, and the Africans show signs of fear.

It is daylight, as I say, and yet we cannot see anything. Wherever we look, the sky is clear. Certainly a fairly lofty hill limits our view just to the east. I hasten towards its summit.

While I am climbing as fast as my legs can carry me, the strange sound increases gradually, then stops suddenly, and by the time I've reached the summit, nothing breaks the silence.

But if I can't hear anything I may be able to see. Before me stretches the plain which, so far as eye can reach, consists of that forest of overgrown grass which forms the bush. The whole stretch is deserted. In vain I strain my eyes, in vain I I stare at the horizon. I can see nothing.

I stay there like a sentry until nightfall. Little by little the dark shadows cover the countryside, for the moon is entering its last quarter and so does not rise until late. It's no use to wait any longer. I go down.

But I'm not half way down when the noise comes again. Really, it's enough to drive one mad. It starts just as it had stopped, suddenly, then decreases gradually, as though it were travelling away eastwards. In a few minutes silence returns.

I complete the descent very thoughtful and go into my tent, where I jot down these few notes.

13th February. A day of rest. Everybody attends to his own affairs.

M. Barsac walks up and down. He seems perturbed.

M. Poncin, under a large tree, is making notes, doubtless referring to his own duties. To judge by the movements of his pencil, he's making some sort of calculation. What calculation? I could ask him, but would he answer? Between ourselves, I'm beginning to fear he's dumb.

St. Bérain. . . . Well, where's St. Bérain got to? I suppose he's off somewhere tackling the fish.

Captain Marcenay is chatting with Mlle Mornas. Don't let's disturb them.

At the other end of the camp, Tongané is accompanying Malik. They, too, don't seem to find the time too long.

The native personnel is sleeping here and there, and except for the sentries the escort is doing the same.

As for myself, I spend a good part of the day finishing an article, aided by my notes.

The article finished and signed, I call Tchoumouki, dedicated to the service of the post. Tchoumouki does not reply. I ask a Tirailleur to go and look for him. Half an hour later, the man returns and says he cannot find him. I hunt for him with no more success. Tchoumouki has vanished and I must give up hoping to send off my article.

14th February. To-day, something spectacular happens.

Towards eight, for we'd spent part of the morning looking for Tchoumouki, we are thinking of going off without him when, towards the west, and so towards Bama which we left two days ago, we see a large troop appearing in the distance.

Captain Marcenay sees it before I do, and gives the necessary orders. In the twinkling of an eye our escort are at their fighting stations.

These precautions are needless. We are not slow to recognize French uniforms, or at least those appropriate to this country; and, when the unknown troop is nearer we see that it consists of twenty regular soldiers of the negro race, all mounted and armed with service rifles, and three Europeans, also on horseback—two N.C.O's and a lieutenant wearing the uniform of the Colonial Infantry.

One of our sergeants is sent to meet the new-comers, who send one of their own on ahead. The two envoys exchange a few words; then the troop, which has halted during the discussion, resumes its march towards us.

It enters our camp, rifles slung, and the lieutenant in command comes up to Captain Marcenay. The following dialogue reaches my ears.

"Captain Marcenay?"

"Yes, Lieutenant. . . ."

"Lieutenant Lacour, of the 72nd Colonial Infantry, at present commanding a mounted detachment of Soudanese Volunteers. I have come from Bammako, Captain; and from beyond Sikasso, where I missed you by a few days, I have been following you."

"What for?"

"Here is a despatch which will tell you, Captain."

Captain Marcenay takes the letter. As he reads it, I observe that his face exhibits mingled surprise and disappointment.

"Very good, Lieutenant. Let me inform M. Barsac and his companions. Then I shall be at your service."

Captain Marcenay takes the letter and comes over to us.

"I have to advise you of some astounding news, Monsieur le Deputé. I have to leave you."

"To leave us!"

That exclamation, truth forces me to say, was made by Mlle Mornas. I look at her. She has turned quite pale and is biting her lips. If I did not know the firmness of her character, I should swear she was going to cry.

We are all bowled over, except for M. Barsac, whose anger overpowers him.

"What's the meaning of this, Captain?" he asks.

"The meaning, Monsieur le Deputé, is that I have formal orders to report to Timbuctoo."

"This is unthinkable!" cries M. Barsac, who seems deeply wounded.

"But it is so," replies the captain. "Please read this."

He hands M. Barsac the despatch which the lieutenant brought him. As the Chief of the Mission runs his eyes over it, he shows repeated signs of indignation; then he passes the letter to us so that we can be witnesses to its unceremonious nature.

I take care to be the last to have it, so that I can jot down a copy:

REPUBLIQUE FRANÇAISE

GOUVERNEMENT GÉNÉRAL DU SÉNÉGAL

CERCLE DE BAMMAKO

LE COLONEL

Order to Captain Pierre Marcenay and to his detachment to report by forced marches to Ségou-Sikoro and so by way of the Niger to Timbuctoo, where he will place himself under the command of the colonel commanding the district. The horses of Captain Marcenay's detachment will be left in the stables at Ségou-Sikoro.

Lieutenant Lacour, of the 72nd Regiment of Colonial Infantry, commanding a mounted detachment of 20 Soudanese Volunteers, will take this order to Captain Marcenay, at Sikasso, and place himself in the service of M. le Deputé Barsac, Chief of the Extra-parliamentary Mission of the Niger Bend (First Section), whom he will escort to his destination.

Colonel Commanding le Cercle de Bammako,

SAINT-AUBAN

While I am feverishly copying this, M. Barsac goes on breathing out his bad temper.

"It's unspeakable!" he says. "To give us an escort of twenty strong . . . and just when we've run up against our greatest difficulties! . . . But this won't be the last of it. . . . The moment I get back to Paris, we shall see if the Chamber approves of one of its Members being treated so charmingly!"

"But meantime we have to obey." Captain Marcenay said, not even trying to conceal his distress.

M. Barsac takes the captain aside, but I have a reporter's ear and I can hear quite well.

"Captain, the order may not be genuine!" he suggests in low tones.

The captain starts. "Not genuine!" he repeats. "You need not think that, Monsieur le Député. Unfortunately there's no doubt about it. The letter bears all the official seals. Besides I've served under Colonel Saint-Auban, and I know his signature quite well."

Bad temper can excuse much, but I think M. Barsac is going too far. Fortunately Lieutenant Lacour has not heard him. He would not feel flattered.

M. Barsac has nothing to reply and keeps silence.

"Would you allow me, Monsieur le Député, to introduce Lieutenant Lacour and then take my leave?"

M. Barsac having agreed, the introductions are made.

"Do you know, Lieutenant," M. Barsac asks him, "the reasons for the order you have brought?"

"Certainly, Monsieur le Député," replies the lieutenant. "The Touareg Aouelimmeden are astir and they are threatening our lines. Hence the need to reinforce the garrison at Timbuctoo. The Colonel is using whatever comes to hand."

"What about us?" asks the chief of the Mission. "Is it prudent to cut our escort down to twenty men?"

Lieutenant Lacour smiles.

"There will be no difficulty about that," he assures him. "This region is absolutely quiet."

"That's not so certain," M. Barsac objects. "The Minister for the Colonies himself has reported to the tribune of the Chamber, and the Resident at Konakry has confirmed it—that the regions near the Niger are the scene of some very disquieting events?"

"That used to be true enough," replies Lieutenant Lacour, still smiling, "but there's no question of it now. That's ancient history."

"But we ourselves have found. . . ." M. Barsac insists, and he tells the lieutenant about our own adventures.

That does not seem to disturb him.

"But you must see," he replies, "that this unknown antagonist, who seems to preoccupy you beyond all reason, must be a very insignificant person after all. What! he wants, you say, to bar your route, and yet he couldn't think up any way of stopping you? . . . You can't be serious, Monsieur le Deputé."

M. Barsac has nothing to say.

Captain Marcenay comes up. "Permit me, Monsieur le Deputé, to take my leave," he says.

"What! So soon!" cries M. Barsac.

'I must,' the captain replies. "My orders are formal. I must reach Segou-Sikoro and Timbuctoo without losing an hour."

"Then do so, Captain," M. Barsac agrees, holding out his hand, his feelings overcoming his anger, "and be sure you are taking all our good wishes with you. None of us will forget the time we have spent together, and I know I'm speaking for all of us when I say how fully we realize the vigilant protection and unfailing devotion you have shown."

"Thank you, Monsieur le Deputé," replies the captain; he also is deeply moved.

He takes farewell of each of us in turn, ending, as goes without saying, with Mlle Mornas. As might be supposed, I look at them out of the corner of my eye.

But I get little for my curiosity. Everything goes off the simplest thing in the world.

"*Au revoir*, Mademoiselle," says the captain.

"*Au revoir,* Captain," replies Mlle Mornas.

Nothing more. Nevertheless, for those who are in the secret, these few words have a special significance. We realize that they are the equivalent of a mutual and formal promise.

Thus I understand the captain, whose face has regained its calm. He takes the hand which Mlle Mornas holds out to him, respectfully presses a kiss on it, goes away, leaps on his horse, and takes his place at the head of his detachment, which has meantime formed up.

A last salute in our direction, then he raises his sabre. The hundred men move off and break into a trot. Not without some distress, we follow them with our eyes. In a few minutes they are out of sight.

There we are alone with Lieutenant Lacour, his two N.C.O's and his twenty men, whose very existence we did not even suspect an hour ago. The episode has taken place so quickly we are quite stunned. Now we have to regain our calm.

I regain mine fairly quickly, and I look at our new bodyguard, so as to get to know them. Then something strange happens. At the first glance I throw over them, I feel a slight shiver—not unpleasant, my word, no—for I suddenly get the definite impression that they seem to be the sort of people whom I would not like to find myself with at the corner of a wood.

CHAPTER X

THE NEW ESCORT

(*From the notebook of Amédée Florence*)

Same day, evening. No, I should not like to find myself with them at the corner of a wood, and yet here I am—or rather I'm with them in the middle of the bush, which is far worse. So the situation is charming. To know you're running into danger, but not what it is; to be always trying to guess what it is that is hiding from you; eye and ear always alert to ward off the blow you apprehend, without knowing whence it will come—nothing could be more "exciting." It's during such hours that one lives really intensively, and these sensations nicely supplant the pleasure of a coffee with cream on a Parisian terrace.

Let's get on! There I am, running on in my usual style. In representing our escort as bandits when no doubt they're quite ordinary Tirailleurs, isn't my imagination playing me a nasty trick? And the letter, the authentic letter from Colonel Saint-Auban, what am I to make of that?

Whatever I wish, that letter is a difficulty, I agree, but nothing can prevail against my impression of our new escort and its commander.

First of all, that officer, those N.C.O's, those soldiers, are they military? Regarding the Africans, nobody can tell. For the officer, one is inclined to say "yes." On the other hand, one would reply no without hesitation regarding the two sergeants. Tirailleurs, with heads like that? Tell that to someone else! No need to be a phrenologist, or a physiognomist, nor any other scholarly ist, to read in those faces the uneasiness of the trapped beast, the love of gross pleasures, uncontrolled violence and cruelty. A charming portrait!

What first struck me is only a detail, but it opened the tap of my cogitations. Isn't it indeed strange that these men, the

N.C.O's included, should be covered with dust like people who've been chasing us for a fortnight, while their leader is as fresh as if he'd come out of a band-box?

For he is fresh, and to a most improbable degree. Clean linen, shining boots, waxed moustache, he's quite a pretty boy. And his deportment? Anyone would think that Lieutenant Lacour were going to hold a review. He is regimental from head to toe. Nothing is amiss, not a button, not a thread, down to his trousers, with a crease as if they were brand-new. You don't often get the chance, in the bush, of admiring such elegance. That uniform announces to all comers that it has never before been worn, that it's quite new, and that the man who wears it is so anxious to look like an officer that he's gone beyond the limits of probability.

With so much spit and polish when his subordinates are so dusty? Hasn't Lieutenant Lacour done as much chasing about as they have?

The two sergeants, on the other hand, are very dirty; but if they haven't got the exaggerated elegance of their officer, they sin, to my mind, by too much of the opposite. Their uniforms (?) look like reach-me-downs. They are in rags. The trousers are much too large and too much patched, and no number, no symbol, indicates the regiment.

I can hardly believe that French soldiers would be allowed to get into such a state. Something else more difficult to express: I feel as if the men who wear these old uniforms are not used to wearing them. Although I can't quite explain why, they haven't the air of being at home in them.

Such are my observations. They may seem inadequate, and I may be very wrong in letting myself be swayed by such trifling details, which may have the simplest explanation in the world. I won't say no, for I'm not far from that opinion myself. In seeking to define, to set down in writing, the reasons for my distrust, I'm the first to admit their weakness. But this distrust is first and foremost a matter of instinct, and I can't put it into words.

As regards discipline, there's nothing to say. Indeed, to my mind it's rather too strict. The sentries on watch relieve one another regularly. The general routine is perfect, perhaps too perfect.

The escort is divided sharply into three groups, none of whom are on good terms with the convoy. The first consists of the twenty Soudanese Tirailleurs. Outside their hours of guard duty, they hang together and, an incredible thing among Africans, they scarcely ever speak. They prepare their meals in silence, or they sleep. We never hear anything from them. They obey the merest glance of their N.C.O's, whom they seem to fear greatly. It looks, indeed, as if these twenty negroes are thoroughly unhappy and thoroughly scared.

The second group comprises the N.C.O's. These do speak, but only to one another, and always under their breath. Even my reporter's ear has not been able, so far, to catch a single word of importance.

The third and last group consists of Lieutenant Lacour all by himself. He is a man of small stature, who does not impress me as a very attractive gentleman. He has pale blue eyes, steely eyes as they say, which do not exactly express a universal benevolence. Not talkative, and unsociable into the bargain. Throughout the afternoon, I have only seen him come out of his tent twice, and then simply to inspect his men.

This operation does not vary. As soon as they see their chief, the Tirailleurs jump to their feet and line up. The lieutenant, stiff as a ramrod, inspects them, while his frozen glance runs over them from head to feet; then he disappears into his quarters, without saying a word to anyone. Even at the most favourable, I dare say that this elegant officer will not be, to say the least, a cheerful companion.

Throughout the day, I have not seen Mlle Mornas.

Nor Tchoumouki either, which means that I still have my article in my pocket.

15th February. At reveille this morning, I observe no

preparations for our departure. I ask Tongané, who tells me that we are not going to budge all day. After yesterday's rest, this halt seems strange.

By chance I run into Lieutenant Lacour, always erect and still faultlessly elegant. I stop him and ask the reason for this supplementary halt.

"M. Barsac's orders," he replies laconically.

Three words, after which he gives a military salute and turns on his heels. Lieutenant Lacour is not what one calls a conversationalist.

Why is the Chief of the Mission marking time like this? Does he mean to give up his journey now the escort is cut down by four-fifths? This intrigues me. It disquiets me too, because that decision would bring to an end a reportage which seems on the point of becoming sensational.

Exactly at ten I see M. Barsac. He steps out, his hands behind his back and his eyes turned towards the earth, and he doesn't seem in a good humour. This moment is perhaps not well-chosen for asking him about his plans. However, I risk the interview.

M. Barsac does not get annoyed. He stops, and looks at me for a time in silence. At last he says: "It's only a few days, Monsieur Florence, since you asked me the same question. I did not answer. I will answer to-day that I do not know myself."

"Then you haven't come to any decision, Monsieur le Deputé."

"None; I ponder, I fumble, I weigh the pros and the cons...."

Again silence, then suddenly: "But in fact," M. Barsac exclaims, "why shouldn't we go into the question together? You are a practical fellow, full of good sense." (Thank you, Monsieur Barsac) "I should like your opinion."

I bow: "At your service, Monsieur le Deputé."

"Let us first consider whether the journey can be continued without imprudence."

I suggest: "It might first be better to ask whether it's any use."

"Not at all," replies M. Barsac. "Its value is certain."

I am taken aback. However, M. Barsac continues: "Then is the journey feasible? That is the problem. Until yesterday the question did not arise, for so far no really serious incident has marked our path. Isn't that your view?"

"Quite."

"The first incident of any real importance is this unforeseen alteration in our escort, its being cut down to twenty men. Can twenty men assure our safety in the midst of this negro population? That's what I want to know."

"Put in those terms," I say, "the question only admits of an affirmative reply. I feel sure that twenty men will be quite enough, if the only enemies we meet are to be negroes. Other explorers have made longer journeys than ours with a smaller escort, or with no escort at all. But...."

"I know what you're going to say," M. Barsac breaks in. "You're going to mention this mysterious unknown person who doesn't seem to want to have us in his country. I haven't concealed my views regarding this, and the others have agreed. Nothing fresh has happened since. So to my mind it's useless to go over it again."

I reply. "Forgive me, Monsieur le Deputé, but on the other hand, I think there is something new."

"Bah!" M. Barsac is surprised. "Something new that's been kept from me? Explain yourself!"

Thus cornered, I can't help feeling embarrassed. My notes, which seemed so important, and their results, which I thought so logical, seem, now that I have to put them into words, more insignificant and arbitrary than when I jotted them down. But, as I've foolishly started the hare—as was my duty, anyhow—I've got to chase it.

I do chase it. I disclose to M. Barsac my observations on our escort and the officer who commands it, and I end by timidly putting forward the hypothesis that if these gentry aren't real soldiers they may well be in the pay of that unknown adversary whom so far we haven't taken seriously.

When he hears these enormities, M. Barsac starts laughing.

"What a romance!" he exclaims. "Monsieur Florence, I think you've got a wonderful imagination. You will find this very useful if ever you go in for the theatre, but I advise you to steer clear of it in real life."

"However...." I say, annoyed.

"It isn't a matter of 'however'. Look at the facts. First of all, that order in writing...."

"It might be false."

"No," replies M. Barsac, "for Captain Marcenay regarded it as authentic and obeyed it without hesitation."

"It might have been stolen...."

"Another romance! How, I ask you, could a substitute be found for the real escort? They would have to hold in readiness a troop strong enough first to wipe out the escort to the last man—to the last man, you understand—and then to substitute a spurious detachment absolutely identical with them. And all this a long way in advance, when nobody could possibly know what the new escort would be, or even whether Colonel Saint-Auban would send it off.

"As none of Lieutenant Lacour's men has been wounded, that troop would have to be very strong, for you will concede, I suppose, that the original escort would not have let themselves be massacred without putting up a fight? And you have it that so strong a band would not be noticed, that the rumour of such a fight would not have reached us although in the bush news flies from village to village as fast as a telegram? See what impossibilities you're up against when you let your imagination run riot!"

M. Barsac is right. The order can't have been stolen. He goes on:

"As for your impression of the men and their leaders, what do you base that on? How are these Tirailleurs, whom you see in front of you, different from any other black Tirailleurs?"

I look at them, and I'm forced to recognize that he is right again. Where were my wits yesterday evening? I've been a victim of auto-suggestion. These negroes are just like any other negroes.

M. Barsac realizes his advantage. He continues with even more assurance (and God knows whether it's assurance he lacks!)

"Let's get on to the N.C.O.'s. What do you find so special about them? They're very dirty, it's true, but no worse than some of Captain Marcenay's sergeants. On active service you really can't be so punctilious about the state of their uniforms."

He's got a golden eloquence. I put in a word timidly, for I'm really shaken: "But Lieutenant Lacour...."

"Oh, that's a queer complaint," exclaims M. Barsac, smiling. "He's clearly meticulous about his person and toilet. That's not a crime."

No, it isn't. I make a last effort and suggest: "All the same, a uniform shrieking that it's new—that's queer!"

"Because his other uniform is in his kit-bag," M. Barsac explains; he has an answer for everything. "It must be covered with dust and Monsieur Lacour wanted to look his best before displaying himself to us."

M. Barsac seems to find that very natural. Perhaps, after all, it is I who do not quite realize the importance of the Chief of the Mission.

"Besides, I've had a long talk with Lieutenant Lacour, yesterday afternoon. He's a delightful man, although he likes to overdo his elegance, I quite agree. Polite, well educated, deferential, even respectful."

At this point M. Barsac throws out his chest.

"Even respectful. I think he's a very pleasant companion and a willing subordinate."

I ask: "Doesn't the lieutenant see any difficulty in continuing our journey under these conditions?"

"None at all."

"And yet you're doubtful, Monsieur le Deputé."

"I shall hesitate no longer," declares M. Barsac, who has convinced himself while he was talking. "We shall start tomorrow."

"Without even wondering whether it's useful now that we've settled it's possible?"

The gentle irony of my question goes unnoticed.

"What for?" asks M. Barsac. "This journey is not only useful, it is *essential*."

"Essential?"

Restored to his good humour, M. Barsac takes me familiarly by the arm and explains in confidential tones:

"Between ourselves, my dear fellow, I'm willing to agree that the Africans whom we've recently met are far from being advanced enough to become voters. I will agree, too, if you insist, that we have no chance of being more fortunate so long as we turn our backs on the coast. But though I'm telling this to you, I shouldn't say so at the tribune of the Chamber.

"Now, if we complete our journey, things will go on as follows: Baudrières and I will put in reports whose conclusions are diametrically opposed, and these reports will be considered by a Commission. Then either we shall make mutual concessions, and the vote will be given to some of the natives on the coast, which will be a victory for me, or else we shan't make any concessions, and the matter will be dropped. A week later, nobody will be thinking about it any more, and nobody will ever know whether the facts showed me right or wrong. Either way, nothing will keep either Baudrières or myself, whichever way the wind blows, from one day having the portfolio of the Colonies. But if I should return without accomplishing my Mission, that would be to announce publicly that I'd lost my way: my enemies would shout at the top of their voices that I was nothing but an old fool, and I should be sunk once and for all."

M. Barsac makes a slight pause, then concludes with this profound thought: "Never forget this truth, M. Florence:

anyone in politics can make a mistake. That doesn't matter. But if he admits his error, he's lost."

I savour this maxim, and I go away satisfied. I am quite satisfied, indeed, for at last I understand the motives of us all.

After leaving M. Barsac I happen to come across M. Poncin's note-book, which he has chanced to leave on a folding-chair. My journalistic instincts triumph over my good manners, and I deliberately open it. I've been wondering about this for a long time, what our silent companion keeps writing from morning to night.

Alas! I'm well punished for my curiosity. It's nothing but a tangle of incomprehensible figures and letters mixed up at random: "p.j. 0.009," "p.k.c. 135.08," "M. 76.18" and so forth.

Another mystery! Why this secret writing? Has M. Poncin something to hide? Is he betraying us, too?

There we are, on my hobby-horse again. I must look out for that. What an idea, to suspect this good fellow! That's paying him too much honour, because—I can say it to this note-book simply for my own benefit—he hasn't enough sense, our M. Poncin.

But either you are a journalist or you're not. I copy a few random examples of these hieroglyphics.

I put the note-book back and go off with my booty. Perhaps that will be enough. One never knows.

During the afternoon, a ride. I go out along with Tongané, who has taken Tchoumouki's horse, which is better than his own. We go off into the country at a gentle trot. After five minutes, Tongané, whose tongue is itching, suddenly says: "It be good Tchoumouki get out. Tchoumouki dirty black rascal. Him traitor."

Well here's another of them! What! Tchoumouki betraying us, too? I know that this is the time to verify things. I pretend to be surprised.

"That's Moriliré that you're talking about."

"Moriliré, him no good," Tongané says with energy. "But Tchoumouki same thing Moriliré. Negroes say 'Him no good walk!' give much *dolo toubab* (brandy), much money, much gold."

Gold in the hands of Moriliré and Tchoumouki? That isn't likely!

"You mean that they give the negroes cowries, to get them round?"

"Not cowries," Tongané insists. "Much gold."

And he adds a detail which bowls me over: "Much gold English."

"You know English gold then, Tongané?"

"*Ioo*," the negro tells me. "Me Ashanti. Me know *pounshterlings*."

I realize that by this singular word Tongané means "pounds sterling." It's a queer word. I have tried to transcribe it in phonetic writing but in Tongané's mouth it sounds better. But now I don't feel like laughing. Gold!—and English gold!—in the hands of Tchoumouki and Moriliré! . . . I'm bowled over. However, I don't let this appear, and pretend not to attach any importance to the news.

"You are a good fellow, Tongané. I tell my companion and as you know *pounshterlings* so well, take this little gold piece with the picture of the French Republic."

"Him good Republic!" cries Tongané. Overcome with delight, he throws the piece I offer him into the air, catches it in its flight and thrusts it into one of the saddle-bags.

At once a look of astonishment crosses his face, and he pulls from the opening a thick roll of paper—an object hardly likely to be found among the negroes. I give a cry and snatch out of his hand a script which I recognize at once.

My articles! They're my articles! My wonderful articles waiting in the saddle-bags of that rascal Tchoumouki! Alas! All of them are there, beginning with the fourth. How harshly they'll judge me at *L'Expansion Française!* I shall be dishonoured, and lose my reputation for ever!

While I ponder these sad thoughts, we keep travelling on at a gentle trot. We must be a little over three miles from the camp when I stop suddenly. I have just come across something very strange.

It is almost on the edge of the road, a space six or seven yards wide and almost fifty yards long, marked out in the midst of the bush. Over that space the tall grass is lying flat, crushed, part of it even cut short as if by a gigantic scythe. Moreover—and this especially attracts my attention—in the ground thus laid bare we can clearly see two parallel grooves, like those which we noticed near Kankan, about four inches deep at on end and petering out at the other. This time the deep end is towards the east.

In spite of myself I have to associate these deeply-cut grooves with the roaring we heard the other evening. It was at Kankan, too, that we heard that strange roaring before we noticed those inexplicable marks on the ground.

What connection is there between these two phenomena—the roaring, the pairs of grooves—and the *Kéniélala* of Kankan? I can't see any. Yet this connection must exist: while I'm wondering about these enigmatical furrows, my subconscious spontaneously calls up the ugly face of the negro sorcerer. And how that face looks to me now that, of the four predictions of the old humbug, the third, after two of the others, has just been fulfilled!

There, alone with my black companion in the immensity of the desert, a cold shiver—the second, counting the one I felt yesterday—runs down my back from head to heels, and for a moment, thinking of the mystery which surrounds me, I feel afraid.

It's agonizing, especially in such conditions. Yet it does not last, because I'm not much addicted to fear. My own weakness is curiosity. So, while we're going back, I go again and again over these irritating problems which I have to solve, and make myself dizzy looking for the answer. This exercise absorbs me so much that I hardly notice what's around me.

When we reach the camp, I jump. Tongané, without the slightest warning, suddenly says:

"*Toulatigui* (lieutenant) him no good. Dirty monkey head."

I answer without thinking, and that must be my excuse: "That's it!"

17th February. A long march to-day, and longer still yesterday. Thirty miles in two days! Tchoumouki hasn't come back —the swine!—nobody has seen him. Guided only by Tongané, our muleteers and porters are doing marvellously and stepping out as briskly as they can.

I must admit that during these two days my misgivings have rather died away. The escort has been strictly attending to its duties, though these are not very onerous. The twenty men, in two files, flank the convoy, just like those of Captain Marcenay. The only thing I notice is that they do not exchange with our black personnel the jokes of the same colour of which their predecessors were not sparing. That, however, does honour to their discipline.

The two N.C.O's, when they are not moving up and down the line of Tirailleurs, usually stay with the rear-guard. They do not speak to anyone except their men, to whom every now and again they give curt orders which are obeyed instantly. If our escort is not strong, it is at least firmly commanded.

Lieutenant Lacour goes at the head, almost in the place which Captain Marcenay used to take, beside M. Barsac. I notice that Mlle Mornas has fallen back a few paces. She stays with St. Bérain, behind Dr. Châtonnay and M. Poncin. She doesn't look as if she much values the lieutenant's company.

There is little to say about him, however. If he doesn't speak, he acts. Certainly his attitude is not entirely unconnected with the satisfactory result of these two days' march.

No, nothing to say. And yet....

But, that must be a fancy of my own. The mystery I feel around me, the weird facts which I've observed, are troubling my mind, and I'm inclined, perhaps too much inclined, to see treachery everywhere.

Whatever it may be, this is what arouses my misgivings.

It was this morning, about nine. We were going through a

little village which was completely deserted when we heard groans coming from one of the huts.

On M. Barsac's orders, the convoy stops and Dr. Châtonnay, accompanied by Lieutenant Lacour and two Tirailleurs, goes into the hut. Needless to say the Press, in the person of myself, goes in with them.

There a sad spectacle meets our eye. There are two dead bodies, and a wounded man. A frightful thing—the two corpses, a man's and a woman's, are horribly mutilated! Who has killed and wounded these poor people? Who can be guilty of these atrocious mutilations?

Dr. Châtonnay at once deals with the wounded man. As it is so dark in the hut, he orders two of the Tirailleurs to carry him out. He is an oldish negro. He has been injured in the shoulder, and the wound is terrible. The collar-bone is exposed. I wonder what weapon could have caused such damage.

The doctor cleans up the wound and extracts numerous fragments of lead. He brings the flesh together, puts in some stitches, and carefully dresses the wound, while Lieutenant Lacour helps him by handing him the dressings. Throughout the whole operation, the patient never stops giving heart-rending groans. He seems to be suffering less when the treatment is finished.

But the doctor seems anxious. He goes a second time into the hut and examines the two corpses, and when he comes out he is more anxious still. He goes up to the sufferer, whom he interrogates with the help of Tongané.

From the poor negro's story, it appears that, six days ago—that would be the 11th, three days before our escort was changed—the tiny village had been attacked by a party of negroes led by two white men. Except for the man and woman whose corpses we had found and who hadn't had time to take cover, the inhabitants had fled into the bush. The wounded man had been with the others. Unfortunately, while he was running away a shot had hit him in the shoulder, but he none the less had time to hide himself, and so he had escaped. Later his companions had brought him back to the village, but everybody had again taken flight when they saw another troop coming, exactly from the direction in which the first had gone.

Such was his story, and it did not fail to disquiet us. It can't be very pleasant, indeed, to learn that a horde of such miscreants is roaming about the country. It was only by sheer luck, indeed, that we hadn't run into them when they were coming towards us.

However, the poor devil was expressing gratitude to Dr. Châtonnay when suddenly he fell silent, while his eyes showed the greatest terror and fixed their stare on someone or something behind us. We looked round, and found ourselves face to face with one of our two N.C.O.'s; it was the sight of him which had so frightened the negro.

The N.C.O. didn't seem troubled. He seemed troubled enough, however, when the frozen eyes of Lieutenant Lacour sent him a message of reproach and menace. I caught a glimpse of this glare, which I am unable to explain. The sergeant simply touched his head, to indicate that the sufferer was delirious, and went off to rejoin his men.

We went back to our patient. But the spell was broken. He looked at us terrified, and we couldn't get another word out of him. He was carried back into his hut and we went off, partly reassured as to his fate, for Dr. Châtonnay says his wounds will heal.

I don't know what my companions made of it. For my part, as we went on, I dug into this new problem. Why had the old negro shown so much fear? Why, when he had paid no attention to Lieutenant Lacour, had this terror been aroused—there was no doubt of this—by the sight of one of our sergeants?

For a change, there is no solution to this problem. All these insoluble riddles with which chance perplexes us end by being disquieting.

This evening, fairly late, we pitch our tents near a little

village called Kadou. We are sorry to reach it, for it was at Kadou that Mlle Mornas and St. Bérain were to leave us. While we were going straight on towards Ouaghadougou and the Niger, they would push on northwards, with Gao and that same Niger as their objective.

Needless to say how all of us try to make them give up this insane project. Our efforts were in vain. I dare to forecast that the future better-half of Captain Marcenay will not be very amenable. When Mlle Mornas has got an idea into her head, the devil himself couldn't get it out!

In despair, we ask the help of Lieutenant Lacour and beg him to explain to our fair companion the folly she was about to commit. I am sure his efforts would have been thrown away, but he didn't take the trouble to make them. He made an evasive gesture and smiled—with a smile which I thought rather queer, but I can't exactly say why.

So we halt near Kadou. Just as I am about to retire to my tent, Dr. Châtonnay calls me back. He says: "One thing I want to tell you, Monsieur Florence, is that the bullets which struck those negroes that day were explosive."

And he goes off without waiting for my reply.

Well! Another mystery! Explosive bullets now! Who can use such weapons? How, indeed, can such weapons exist in this country?

Two more riddles to add to my collection, which never stops growing. On the other hand, it's my collection of answers which never gets bigger!

18th February. The very latest news, without comment. Our escort has gone. I say it's gone completely.

I insist because this is quite incredible, and I repeat: our escort is gone. When we got up, three or four hours ago, we could not find them. They had evaporated, gone off like smoke during the night, and with them had gone all the porters and muleteers without exception.

Is that clear? Lieutenant Lacour, his two sergeants and his twenty men, had not gone out for their morning constitutional.

meaning to get back for lunch. They're gone, de-fin-it-ive-ly gone.

Here we are alone in the bush, with our horses, our personal weapons, thirty-six donkeys, provisions for five days and Tongané!

Well, I wanted adventures. . . .

CHAPTER XI

WHAT'S TO BE DONE?

WHEN the members of the Barsac Mission realized as they awoke at Kadou on the 18th February that their escort and their black personnel had vanished, they were stunned. So extraordinary was this twofold defection, especially that of the escort, that for a while they could not believe it. But then came evidence that soldiers and servants were gone never to return.

Amédée Florence had broken the news to the others, who quickly gathered together. Naturally, the discussion was at first desultory, a matter of exclamations rather than of thoughts. Plans for the future are always preceded by expressions of astonishment at the present.

A groan from an adjacent thicket showed them that they were not as alone as they supposed. They ran to the place whence the groaning seemed to come and there they found Tongané bound, gagged, and, moreover, wounded in the side.

When he had been freed, revived, and given first aid, he was questioned. Half in his native tongue, half in Bambara, he told them what he had seen of the desertion.

Aroused early that morning by some unexpected noises, Tongané had been surprised to see the twenty Tirailleurs on horseback and moving away. Meantime, the black personnel, directed by Lieutenant Lacour and the two sergeants, were astir and seemed busy with some task which he could not clearly see. Interested, and so far unsuspicious, he had got up and approached them to find out what they were doing.

He never reached them. Half-way across, he had been pounced on by two men, one of whom had gripped him by the throat without giving him time to utter a word. In a moment he was thrown to the ground, gagged, bound. But he was able to see that the Africans, porters and muleteers alike, were being loaded with numerous packages.

Having thus rendered Tongané helpless, his assailants were making off, when Lieutenant Lacour asked curtly: "That settled?"

"Yes," replied one of the sergeants.

There was a brief silence. Tongané felt that someone was bending over him. Hands were moving over his body, were feeling him.

"But you are fools, I tell you," said the lieutenant. "You're going off and leaving a rascal who may have seen too much. Robert, kindly stick a bayonet into this vermin."

The order was at once carried out, but Tongané was able to give his body a twist. Instead of piercing him in the chest, the weapon simply slid along his side, so that the wound was spectacular rather than serious. In the darkness, the lieutenant and his two acolytes were deceived, especially as the astute guide had taken the precaution of groaning as though he were rendering up his soul, and then holding his breath; the blood on the bayonet also deceived the assassins.

"That settled?" repeated Lieutenant Lacour, when the blow had been delivered.

"All right!" replied the man called Robert.

The three men had then moved away and Tongané had heard nothing else. Soon he lost consciousness, partly because of the gag which stifled him, partly because of his loss of blood. He knew no more.

This made it clear that it was a question not of a temporary absence of the escort but of a premeditated desertion.

That point settled, the explorers looked at each other, stupefied and overcome with consternation. The first to break the silence was Amédée Florence, for whom the reader's indulgence is again asked.

"Quick work," he exclaimed, expressing the general thought in somewhat familar form.

That comment seemed to release the tension, and soon measures were being taken to meet the situation. First a schedule had to be drawn up: seven guns, including six for hunting, ten revolvers, plenty of ammunition, seven horses, thirty-six donkeys, about 1,000 pounds of trade-goods and provisions for four days. So there was no lack of means of defence and transport, and there was no need to worry about provisions, for it would be easy to get them in the villages, as hitherto; hunting would moreover be possible. So wherever they might end up, the party would not be hindered, from the material point of view, by any insuperable obstacle.

First the donkeys, which would be a serious hindrance without experienced muleteers, had to be got rid of. Then a plan was drawn up. If they decided to push on any distance, they would try to hire five or six porters, to carry the trade-goods which they could exchange in the villages for the provisions they would need. Otherwise they would dispose of these at once regardless of cost, to avoid the need for porters and facilitate progress.

Jane Mornas and St. Bérain, the only two who could understand the natives, at once got into touch with the inhabitants of Kadou. They were warmly welcomed in the village, and a few little gifts won the sympathy of the head man, who gave them all the help he could.

Thanks to his aid, the donkeys were sold at about 10,000 cowries (about thirty francs) each, making more than 350,000 cowries in all. This alone would assure for over twenty days the existence of the members of the Mission and the payment of the five porters which the head man was able to supply.

These negotiations took several days, but this time was not wasted, for Tongané could not have been ready to take the road earlier. At last his wound, which was quite superficial, was well on the way to healing.

So, on the morning of the 23rd, six camp-chairs were arranged in a circle with the maps spread out at the centre. Then, with Tongané and Malik for audience, the discussion began under the chairmanship of Barsac.

"The session is open," he said mechanically, like a man used to the protocol of the Chamber. "Who wishes to speak?"

There were concealed smiles. Amédée Florence, somewhat addicted to irony, replied without even a cough: "We'll speak after you, Monsieur le Président."

"As you wish," agreed Barsac, not at all surprised at the title bestowed upon him. "First we must define the situation. We find ourselves abandoned by our escort, but well supplied with weapons and trade goods, right in the Sudan, some distance from the coast."

At these words M. Poncin drew his huge note-book from his pocket, balanced a pince-nez on his nose, and—he who never spoke—he said: "Exactly 880 miles, 938 yards and 1 foot and $4\frac{3}{4}$ inches, reckoned from the centre-post of my tent."

"So much precision isn't needed, M. Poncin," Barsac commented. "Sufficient to say that we are about nine hundred miles from Konakry. As you are not unaware, we planned to go much further but the new situation demands a new solution. To my mind our objective should be to reach, if not most quickly at least most safely, some centre where there is a French post. There we will take council, and we can examine quite calmly what we are to do next."

Agreement was unanimous.

"The map," Barsac continued, "shows that we ought to try to reach the Niger somewhere along its course. Couldn't we make for Saye, by way of Ouaghadougou and Nadiango? Since they captured Timbuctoo, the French posts have never stopped gaining ground down-stream. I don't know, I admit, whether they have got to Saye, but that's possible, I will even say probable. Then if we succeed in obtaining another escort, that will have the advantage of following the programme scheduled."

"But that will have the inconvenience, Monsieur le Président," burst out M. Poncin, feverishly jotting down figures in his note-book, "of demanding a journey of five hundred miles. But our paces, I am informed, are on the average twenty-five inches. Five hundred miles would thus make 1,011,111 paces and a fraction." He continued with a string of figures.

"OH! oh! *oh!*" came a crescendo of exclamations from Amédée Florence, who was on the point of having a nervous breakdown, "couldn't you simply say that it will take fifty-three days at ten miles a day, but only forty if we can make it twelve and a half? What do you expect to get out of these frightful figures?"

"Simply this," M. Poncin replied coldly, putting his impressive note-book away, "that it would be better to reach the Niger by way of Djenné. That would cut the distance down by half, to two hundred and fifty miles."

"This would be better still," Amédée Florence objected, pointing to the map. "Reach the Niger at Segou-Sikoro, going by way of Bama, and so forth. That would be only about a hundred miles. What's more, that centre is fairly large, and we'd be sure to get help there."

"Excellent," Dr. Châtonnay agreed. "All the same, I think we could do better still. Let's just return on our tracks, maybe not to the sea but at any rate to Sikasso, only about a hundred and twenty miles away, where we'll find our fellow-countrymen who welcomed us so warmly. Then we can decide whether to go on to Bammako or, as Monsieur Amédée Florence thinks, and I think too, up to Segou-Sikoro."

"The doctor's right," Florence concurred. "That will be wisest."

"Monsieur Florence," Barsac continued, after a moment's reflection, and wanting to impress his companions with his heroism, "you and the doctor may be right. But I beg you to consider, that returning to Sikasso would show that, for a time at all events, we had abandoned the mission I had accepted. But, gentlemen, a man who puts duty before all...."

"We understand your reluctance, Monsieur Barsac," broke in Florence, who saw where the discourse was tending, "but it's a question not of duty but of prudence."

"It remains to settle," replied Barsac, "exactly what the position is. Our escort has deserted us, certainly, but I vainly ask what dangers menace us. Our only risks have come from some hypothetical adversary—probable I agree but not certain, because we only know about him through the blows he gives us. Consider these blows in themselves, and they will not seem much. What has anyone done except annoy us?

"According to M. Florence, he first tried to scare us; it was again our unknown enemy, I agree, who more recently stirred up trouble with our personnel, and who now has somehow arranged, by some method I can't understand, to palm a false escort off on us. But please remember that he has shown evidence of great moderation. This false escort, instead of merely deserting, could easily have slaughtered us! It has done nothing of the kind. Also it has been thoughtful enough to leave us our provisions, our arms, our ammunition, our mounts, and our merchandise. These proceedings are not very terrible."

"There's Tongané," Dr. Châtonnay pointed out gently.

"Tongané is a negro," Barsac replied, "and for many people the life of a negro doesn't count."

"M. Barsac is right," Florence put in. "Yes, the methods used against us do show signs of a real moderation, and certainly so far nobody has sought our life. I say 'so far,' because our unknown adversary may well take to stronger methods if we keep on going in a direction he dislikes. The way they wounded Tongané is enough to show that those whom we annoy are swift to strike."

"Quite right," the doctor agreed.

Dr. Châtonnay's approval was followed by several minutes' silence, which Barsac spent in profound reflections. Certainly Amédée Florence was right; and most decidedly the Honourable Deputy from the Midi was not going to compromise his precious existence solely to avoid the criticisms awaiting him in Paris, should he return without completing his Mission. But wouldn't it be possible to reply to them?

"All things considered," he said, anxious to try on his audience the arguments he meant to use later on his colleagues of the Chamber, "I support the proposals of M. Amédée Florence, as amended by our honourable colleague, Dr. Châtonnay. I vote, then, for return to Sikasso, with Segou-Sikoro for our final objective. If then, gentlemen...."

Here Amédée Florence, feeling the discourse a little heavy, gave up listening to the orator and thought about something else.

"If then, gentlemen, anyone should seek to blame us for having interrupted this journey unnecessarily, I should reply that the responsibility devolves upon the Government, whose duty was to ensure that our Mission was adequately protected. It should, therefore, when forced to change our escort, have either ensured that a troop of adventurers could not substitute themselves for the detachment assigned to us, or else, if such a substitution has not taken place, to choose a leader with so much integrity that he would not yield to solicitations whose origin it is not our business to see. The enquiry which I demand, the enquiry, gentlemen, will tell us...."

"Pardon, Monsieur?" Amédée Florence interrupted. "If you will allow me...."

The reporter had at first suggested the wisest course, which his practical nature had realized at once. But his proposition ceased to interest him as soon as he realized it was going to be adopted. A few minutes later he ceased to press it because he felt sorry that this journey seemed about to end, just when it promised to become interesting.

At this point his glance happened to fall on two of his companions. He had then interrupted Barsac with as little hesitation as he had ceased to listen to him earlier.

"If you will allow me, M. le Président, I must point out that we are taking our decision without having asked the advice of Mlle Mornas and M. de St. Bérain, who ought, I suppose, to have as much say as ourselves in the debate."

Indeed, while this discussion was going on, the two had listened in silence, without taking any part in it whatever.

"Monsieur Florence is right," Barsac admitted. "If it would please you, Mademoiselle, to let us know your opinion...."

"I thank you for being good enough to consult me," Jane Mornas replied calmly, "but we ought not to join in a discussion which does not concern us."

"Which doesn't concern you? Why not, Mademoiselle? It seems to me we're all flying the same flag."

"Not at all, Monsieur," Jane Mornas replied. "If, through force of circumstances, you renounce your own aim, we have not changed ours. We do not wish to leave you at the very moment when you have so much to distress you, but we have always meant to continue our journey as planned."

"Then you persist in going as far as Gao?"

"More than ever."

"Alone? Without an escort?"

"We never expected anything else."

"With no porters?"

"We shall engage others. If we can't, we shall do without them."

"In spite of this enmity whose origin we don't know but whose reality we can't question?"

"In spite of this enmity, which I think must be aimed rather against you than against us."

"How do you know that, when we've been following the same route? Anyhow it will be against you, I fear, that our unknown enemy will direct his attack, if you go on alone towards the Niger."

"If that is so, we shall brave him."

"But this is madness!" Barsac cried. "If we have to use force we shall not allow you, Mademoiselle, to commit such an imprudence just for the sake of what you yourself call a whim."

Mlle Mornas paused a moment, then replied sadly: "Unfortunately, it's not only a question of a whim."

"What is it a question of, then?" Barsac asked, surprised.

Jane Mornas hesitated again. Then, after a brief silence, she said gravely: "Of duty."

The others looked at her with mixed feelings, wondering

what she meant and what duty could be so imperious as to drag her to the limits of the Niger Bend. But the reporter who, by temperament, had always supposed that his companions had their own reasons for finishing the journey, now felt only a deep satisfaction on realizing that at last he was going to understand the one so far concealed from him.

Jane Mornas continued: "Forgive me, gentlemen, I have deceived you...."

"Deceived us?" Barsac replied, with increasing astonishment.

"Yes, I have been deceiving you. Though M. de St. Bérain has given you his real name and he is as French as you are, I myself have travelled under a false name and a borrowed nationality. I am English, and my name is Jane Blazon. I am the daughter of Lord Blazon and the sister of Captain Blazon, and near Koubo is the last resting-place of my ill-fated brother. So it is there I must go, for there and there alone that I can accomplish the task I have set myself."

Then Jane Blazon—as henceforth she shall be called—described the tragedy of Koubo, the infamous accusation brought against George Blazon, the circumstances of his death, the shame and despair of his father. She explained her sacred task; to rehabilitate her brother, to effect the stain on the family honour, and to restore peace to the old man whose life was ending in the sad loneliness of Uttoxeter Castle.

Her hearers were powerfully gripped by emotion. They could not help admiring this young girl who for such reasons had dared to encounter, and would again encounter, so many fatigues and dangers.

When she had finished: "Miss Blazon," said Amédée Florence, somewhat harshly, "let me lodge a complaint against you."

"A complaint?... Against me?" Jane was amazed, having expected quite a different response.

"Yes, a complaint, and a serious one! What a strange—and not very flattering—opinion have you got, Miss Blazon, of the French in general and of Amédée Florence in particular?"

"What are you trying to say, Monsieur Florence?" stammered Jane, disturbed.

"What!" cried the reporter indignantly, "you thought that Amédée Florence would let you make that little trip to Koubo—without him?"

"Oh, Monsieur Florence. . . ." Jane protested feelingly, as she realized what he meant.

"That's a nice thing!" Amédée Florence went on, pretending to be deeply annoyed. "And how selfish!"

"I don't quite see . . ." Jane began, half smilingly.

"Please let me speak," Florence interrupted her firmly. "So you have forgotten that I am a journalist, and indeed a reporter, and that I've got that strange thing, an editor? Do you know what my editor will say if he hears that I've shirked an assignment so sensational as the Blazon business? Well, he'll say: 'My little Florence, you're nothing but a nincompoop!' And he'll show me the door in two twos. Well, I want to keep my job. So I'm going with you."

"Oh, Monsieur Florence!" Jane repeated; she was deeply moved.

The reporter looked her in the face. "I'm going with you, Miss Blazon," he declared firmly. "And don't waste your time trying to contradict me, for I think I know better than you."

Jane took the gallant fellow's hand: "I accept, Monsieur Florence," she answered, while tears came into her eyes.

"And I, Miss Blazon, will you accept me also?" the deep voice of Dr. Châtonnay suddenly asked.

"You, Doctor?"

"Undoubtedly. Such an expedition cannot dispense with a doctor. As you seem likely to get yourself cut into little pieces, I must be there to sew you up."

"Oh, Doctor," cried Jane, who was beginning to cry.

But what did she feel when she heard Barsac exclaiming in angry tones: "Well, but what about me? I don't count, it seems, for nobody dreams of asking my opinion?"

Barsac was really furious. He too had at once thought of

joining Miss Blazon. He would thus kill two birds with one stone, because the route the girl was to follow resembled his own, and because its imprudence was justified by an aim whose nobility touched him. Moreover, four men, four *Frenchmen,* could they coldly abandon this child in the bush and let her face this hazardous adventure alone? Florence and Dr. Châtonnay had stolen his lines, as they say in the theatre, and that's always unpleasant.

"I'm not speaking for Monsieur Florence," he continued, somewhat exaggerating his real annoyance. "He is a free agent. But as for you, Doctor, you form part of the Mission I'm head of, I suppose. Are you going to be the next to desert, leaving your Chief bereft by the last of his followers?"

"I assure you, Monsieur Barsac . . ." the doctor babbled; he had not thought of this.

"If that wasn't what you meant, Doctor, did you imagine that I too should go on to Koubo? But is it your business to decide what route we're to follow? Above all, is it your business to take the initiative just to keep me in my place?"

"Let me assure you . . ." the poor doctor tried to plead.

"No, Doctor, no, I shall not allow it," replied Barsac, his voice rising gradually. "And understand this that I, the leader responsible for the Niger Mission, do not approve of your plans. On the other hand, considering that the only guide left to us was engaged by Miss Blazon and is solely under her orders, considering that we cannot understand the natives without her help and that of M. de St. Bérain, the only ones who understand their lauguage, I wish, I MEAN, I COMMAND. . . ."

Barsac, whose voice had gained an impressive loudness, paused judiciously then ended more quietly: "That we all make for the Niger by way of Koubo."

"Why, Monsieur Barsac . . ." stammered Jane, fearing she had misunderstood him.

"That's right, Miss Blazon," Barsac cut her short. "You must resign yourself to our company to the end."

"Oh, Monsieur Barsac . . ." she murmured the second time. By now she was crying quite openly.

She was not the only one with moist eyes. The feeling was general. But as the men strove, to conceal it, it somewhat unnerved them and showed itself in a torrent of meaningless words.

"It's quite an easy trip," announced Florence, "for we've got plenty of food."

"For five days," said Dr. Châtonnay, in the same tone as he might have said six months.

"Only four," Barsac corrected him. "But we can buy more."

"Besides, there's hunting," the doctor suggested.

"And fishing," added St. Bérain.

"And fruit, which I'm not quite ignorant of," the doctor agreed.

"Me know plants," Tongané put in a word.

"Me make Cé butter," Malik improved upon him.

"Hip, hip, hip, hurrah!" cried Amédée Florence. "It's Capua, it's the Land of Canaan, it's the Earthly Paradise."

"We shall set off to-morrow," Barsac summed things up. "We must get ready without losing a moment."

It is worth noticing that M. Poncin had not opened his mouth. But as soon as it was decided that they should all go to Koubo, he had taken out his note-book, and was now covering it with endless calculations.

"That's all very well,' he said in response to Barsac's decision. "It's no odds that the Koubo route, compared with that of Segou-Sikoro represents an increase of 250 miles. Our paces being, as is well-known, twenty-five inches, that makes. . . ."

But nobody was listening. The others were already busy getting ready for next day's journey, and M. Poncin was wasting his calculations on the desert air.

CHAPTER XII

THE FOREST GRAVE

Accompanied by six porters provided by the head man, the remnants of the Barsac Mission left Kadou early on the 24th of February. However disquieting the events which had disorganized it, its members were quite cheerful. With the possible exception of M. Poncin, whose feelings were still inscrutable, they were all agreeably over-excited at having accomplished a creditable, indeed almost an heroic, act, and they congratulated one another on their decision.

Moreover, there had been no more losses. Including Tongané, who shared his mount with Malik, they still had their horses, and there was no lack of weapons, provisions, or trade goods. Moreover, the country seemed quiet, and there was reason to hope that the unknown adversary whom they had involuntarily annoyed would bring his persecutions to an end, as the Mission was no longer strong enough to disquiet anyone. They had every hope of reaching Koubo without serious difficulty.

They had every hope, too, of reaching it more quickly, now that they were no longer retarded by a large troop of donkeys, some sure to be obstinate. Still, they had had to make heavy sacrifices. In return for the head man's assistance, they had given him part of their trumpery, though they had enough left to take them to Gao.

A more serious sacrifice was the need to abandon their tents, but they kept one—although she energetically forbade this—for the exclusive use of Jane Blazon. The men would either find shelter in the villages, or sleep in the open; in the dry season, on so short a journey, this would not trouble them greatly. It was only a matter, when all was said and done of travelling about three hundred miles, about fifteen to twenty-days' march. So they should be in Koubo between the 10th and the 15th of March.

The start of the journey harmonized with these favourable auspices. The porters, fresh and full of energy, kept up a good speed, and they took only five days to cross the ninety miles from Kadou to Sanabo, where they arrived on the 28th. No incident marked this part of the journey. As they had expected, they could usually find a night's lodging in the native huts, very dirty indeed but none the less adequate: and the nights in the open air, away from any village, were quite peaceable. Well received everywhere, the travellers got fresh supplies of food without difficulty, and when they left Sanabo on March 1st, they still retained their reserve stores. So far they had no reason to regret the course they had adopted.

"I should say it's too good!" Amédée Florence announced to his friend St. Bérain, as on 2nd March they rode side by side. "The deep thinker whom I'm following may get uneasy about this, and calculate to what fraction the balance-sheet of good and evil has worked out to our benefit. I prefer to think, all the same, that destiny can occasionally model itself on M. Poncin and ignore the odd fractions."

"You see what comes of a good action, my friend," replied St. Bérain. "You didn't want to forsake us, and Heaven will reward you."

"From the way things are going we shan't deserve much," said Dr. Châtonnay, turning round on his saddle.

"Who knows?" asked St. Bérain. "We haven't got there yet."

"Bah!" cried Amédée Florence, "we'll be all right. We've got the wind behind us, this time. I say that we'll arrive at Koubo in an arm-chair, without the slightest adventure to put on record, and that isn't very pleasing to a journalist whose editor . . . Hey there!" he suddenly interrupted himself, speaking to his horse, which had just stumbled heavily.

"What's up?" asked Barsac.

"It's my horse," Florence explained. "He's kept on stumbling all day. I shall have to examine. . . ."

He hadn't time to finish. The horse, which had suddenly

halted, trembled and swayed on its legs. The reporter had barely time to put his foot to the ground, and hardly had he left the saddle when the animal's knees failed, and it fell to earth.

They ran to help the poor beast, which was breathing with difficulty and groaning. They loosened the girth, and moistened its nostrils with water from an adjacent stream. Nothing could be done. Within an hour it was dead.

"I ought to have touched wood just then," lamented Amédée Florence, now become a pedestrian. "Boasting about your luck always brings misfortune, everybody knows that."

"You're superstitious, Monsieur Florence?" Jane Blazon asked smilingly.

"Not exactly, Mademoiselle. Only put out—badly put out in fact."

Tongané's horse was transferred to the reporter and Jane gave a lift to Malik. Then, after a halt of half an hour, they proceeded, leaving the body of the horse and its harness. The march had to be shortened correspondingly.

At nightfall they halted at a clump of trees alongside the road. Situated on a slight rise, so that a look-out could be kept in all directions against the ever-present danger of surprise, this was a good place to spend the night. Certainly its advantages had impressed earlier travellers, who, it soon became clear, had camped at the same spot. To judge by their tracks, they must have been quite numerous and had a number of horses.

Who were these people? Negroes or whites? The latter was the most probable, for negroes do not use horses much. This became a certainty when Amédée Florence found a small object which their predecessors had forgotten. Insignificant in itself, for it was only a button, this was none the less the product of civilization and witnessed irrefutably to its former owner's colour.

The condition of the trampled grass, which was already reviving, showed that their previous journey had taken place at least ten days ago. As they had not met them, the Mission came to the decision that the others were also travelling north-eastwards, so that the two parties were hardly likely to meet.

On the 3rd March, nothing special occurred, but on the 4th the explorers had to mourn another casualty. Towards evening, Barsac's horse died just like that of Amédée Florence. This was beginning to look ominous.

After examining the dead animal, Dr. Châtonnay took the first opportunity of speaking confidentially to Amédée Florence: "I waited till I could be alone with you, Monsieur Florence, to warn you of something serious."

"What's up?" asked Florence surprised.

"Those two horses have been poisoned."

"Impossible!" the reporter cried. "Who would poison them? The blacks we engaged at Kadou? They've no reason to make things difficult for us. On the contrary."

"I'm not accusing anyone," the doctor insisted. "But I stick to my guns. The first death roused my suspicions, and now I'm certain. The signs are unmistakable, and even an ignoramus could not overlook them."

"Well, what's your advice, Doctor?"

"About what?"

"About what we ought to do."

"I don't know any more than you do. My task is to warn you, and if I've done this so confidentially, it's only so that you can pass the word on to the others unknown to Mlle Blazon, for there's no need to alarm her."

"Quite right," Florence agreed. "But tell me, Doctor, do we have to bring malevolence into these two accidents? Mightn't our horses have eaten some poisonous plant along with their provender?"

"That's barely possible, certainly," said the doctor. "It remains to be known whether a poisonous plant got into their food by accident or whether that accident had a human name. On this I know no more than you."

The five remaining horses had to be watched more strictly than ever, to prevent a similar calamity. Someone always kept near them during the halts, so that nobody could approach them without being seen. Whether it was through these precautions, or simply because the two deaths had been accidental, nothing further occurred on the next two days, and the travellers gradually became reassured.

So far these losses had formed the only adverse incident. The country being flat they travelled without fatigue, as fast as the porters could go, and they could still get food quite easily at the villages, so that their supply of four days' provisions remained intact.

However, when the afternoon of the 5th and the morning of the 6th had elapsed without their having seen even one village, they had to break into their reserve. This did not disquiet them, for Tongané was confident that soon they would come to a settlement large enough to supply them with food.

They arrived late on 6th of March at that town, which was called Yaho; but Tongané's promise was not fulfilled. As soon as they neared the *tata,* howls and even a few discharges of flint-locks were heard from its crest, where a crowd of negroes jostled. Apart from the demonstrations at Kokoro, this was the first time they had received such a welcome since they left Konakry. Still, at Kokoro they had been able to turn the warlike reception into more friendly feelings, but at Yaho they could not even attempt this.

In vain Barsac tried to think out some way of getting into touch with the inhabitants; the methods failed one after the other. In vain was a white flag displayed on the end of a stick. This emblem, whose peaceful meaning is known the world over, provoked a storm of howls, accompanied by a shower of musket-balls which would have been fatal to the flag-bearer if he had not been prudent enough to keep at a distance.

Tongané, then two of the porters, were sent as envoys. The people refused to listen, and replied only by a volley of projectiles, rendered inoffensive solely by their clumsy aim. Clearly the population for some reason or other meant to have nothing to do with strangers, and wouldn't even listen to them. The attempt had to be given up.

None the less, these inhospitable fellows confined themselves to guarding the *tata* and delivered no direct act of aggression.

Whatever the reason for their attitude, the travellers could not buy food there as they had hoped; on the next day, the 7th of March, they had to set off with only two days' supply. Yet there was nothing else to disquiet them. They had got over two hundred miles from Kadou, about half the total journey, and had reason to suppose that other villages would be more friendly.

The question could not be settled during the journey of 7th March; this was good as regards distance covered, but now a further mishap occurred. A third horse died, just like the two others.

"Has somebody succeeded in poisoning our animals," Florence asked Dr. Châtonnay, "in spite of the look-out we've kept?"

"That's not very likely," the doctor replied. "The poison must have been administered before we left Kadou, maybe on the very day our escort deserted. True, our horses have died in succession and not all at once, but that may be due to differences of their individual resistance, and no doubt to differences in the doses, too."

"And now," said Amédée Florence, "here we are three pedestrians against four horsemen. That's not so very funny!"

On the 8th, it was not without disquiet that they took to the road: the future was beginning to look black. They could not deny that the adverse power they hoped to have escaped had taken the precaution of poisoning their horses. This suggested a persistent hatred as alarming as it was inexplicable, and every moment they expected to see the surviving animals fall. Moreover, they had only one day's supply of food, and they would soon be suffering from hunger unless they reached another village before sunset.

But they had not to wait so long. Hardly had the first hour of their march elapsed when a group of huts appeared on the skyline.

The travellers stopped a few moments, trying to foresee what sort of welcome awaited them. In the vast plain stretching before their eyes there was nothing to give them any information. So far as they could judge, the village seemed dead and the land deserted. All they could see was the dense carpet of the bush and the groove made by the road; on this they noticed, here and there, dark stains whose nature they could not recognize.

After a short pause, Barsac and his companions continued their march towards the village. They had gone only half a mile when a nauseating smell gripped them by the throat. A few paces further, and they came up to one of the dark stains which they had seen in the distance. They recoiled. It was the decaying corpse of a negro. Right up to the village the road was marked with such bodies—they could count ten of these grim waymarks.

"Look how small a hole that projectile made when it hit the man," said Dr. Châtonnay to Amédée Florence, after examining one of the bodies, "but how large the opening is where it came out. Others have struck a bone, and you can imagine the frightful damage they did. These men were killed by explosive bullets."

"Again!" cried Amédée Florence.

"Again."

"Like that old negro whom we tended during our first march with the new escort?"

"Like him," Dr. Châtonnay replied.

Florence and the doctor rejoined their companions in silence. They were thoughtful, wondering what to infer from this inexplicable repetition of something abnormal enough in itself.

In the village the sight was more frightful still. Numerous

signs indicated that it had been the scene of a furious struggle. Moreover, after the fight the victors had burned it down. In the huts which remained were more of the corpses.

"These wretches perished at least ten days ago," said Dr. Châtonnay, "and like the others they were killed by explosive bullets."

"But who could these wretches be who inflicted this slaughter?" cried St. Bérain.

"Perhaps," suggested Amédée Florence, "the people whose tracks we saw a few days ago. We reckoned they were about ten days ahead of us. That would agree with the time the doctor mentioned."

"We can't doubt that it was them," said Barsac indignantly.

"And it was to them," added Amédée Florence, "that we owe our brusque welcome at Yaho—they must have tried to treat it as they did this. But Yaho is surrounded by a *tata*, so they couldn't get in. That explains why the negroes are frightened and are keeping on the defensive."

"That sounds reasonable," Dr. Châtonnay agreed.

"But who can these wretches be?" asked Jane Blazon, "and mayn't having them near be a danger to us?"

"I don't know who they may be," replied Amédée Florence, "but I don't think we need be afraid of its having anything to do with us. Everything seems to show that they're ten to twelve days ahead, and as they're mounted, it's unlikely we shall ever catch up with them."

They passed through the burnt village without finding any living thing. If all its inhabitants had not been slain by the bullets they had fled, leaving it completely deserted. Moreover, it had been pillaged from end to end. Everything the fire had not consumed had been scattered to the four winds. The same spectacle all around, in the ravaged and devastated *lougans*. The spoilation was obviously deliberate.

They were a prey to the saddest thoughts as they left the unfortunate village. That evening they halted in the open.

They had food only for one meal. They divided it into halves, part to be eaten at once and the rest to be kept for the morning.

On the 9th March they passed two villages. They could not get near the first, as it was protected by a small *tata*, and here they got much the same welcome as at Yaho. The second, which had no fortification, had again been destroyed, pillaged, burned, and bereft of its inhabitants.

"Really one would think," said Barsac, "that they were going out of their way to make a desert before us."

This seemed reasonable. If anyone had wanted to starve the travellers out, they would not have acted otherwise.

"Bah!" said Amédée Florence, deliberately cheerful, "we'll get through this desert in spite of them. It's only about a hundred miles to Koubo. After all, we shan't have to drink the sea! As the butchers and the grocers are on strike, our hunters will provide us with beefsteaks."

Except for M. Poncin, who was quite incapable of handling a gun, they all followed this excellent advice. Unfortunately the tall grass kept them from seeing far, and the country was not at all rich in game. All that day they bagged nothing but a bustard, two guinea-fowl, and two partridges. To feed fourteen people, that was the bare minimum.

After the evening march, Amédée Florence and Dr. Châtonnay realized for the second time that their halting-place had also been visited by others. The grass looked as if it had been trodden down more recently, as if there were a smaller distance between the two parties.

While they were discussing this, Tongané, who was looking after the horses, suddenly called them. Two of the animals had just fallen, like the others. Like these, too, nothing could be done to relieve their sufferings, and within an hour they were dead.

Two horses still remained, but not for long, for on the 10th March they too died.

Were the porters frightened by this series of deaths? More

possibly, as that day the hunting had yielded only derisory results, were they afraid of starving? Whatever the reason, they vanished during the night, so on the 11th the six Europeans, Tongané, and Malik found themselves without porters, without horses, and without food.

Then came a moment of natural discouragement, amply explained by their physical weakness. Saddest of all was Jane Blazon, who, feeling responsible for their misfortunes, reproached herself for having dragged her companions into this wretched predicament. She accused herself and besought their pardon.

Amédée Florence realized how needful it was to combat the general depression.

"There's no use talking like that," he told her, in tones of affectionate brutality. "We're not dead yet! If the hunting hasn't been good so far, what about it? It'll be better tomorrow, that's all."

"Don't forget," said Dr. Châtonnay, coming to the reporter's help, "that when they forsook us, our negroes have relieved us from their six stomachs."

"It's all for the best," concluded Florence. "If they hadn't gone, I'd have suggested sending them back to their loving families. I reckon that as things are, nothing could be better."

"Thank you, Monsieur Florence—and you, too, gentlemen," replied Jane Blazon, deeply moved. "You may be sure I shall never forget your kindness nor your devotion."

"No more sentiment," Florence interrupted her. "Nothing is worse before breakfast. If you'll take my advice we'll get on with our hunting, and then we can eat until we've got stomach-ache!"

Unable to transport the baggage without the porters, they had to abandon the last of the tents and the trade goods. Unless they could find shelter in one of the abandoned villages, Jane Blazon would henceforth have to sleep in the open air. The loss of the merchandise did not distress them much. What good would it be now the country was deserted and trade impossible? Besides, if circumstances should change, hadn't they got some gold money?

On the 12th March they traversed another village, where they found nothing but a number of dead negroes. The doctor pointed out that they had died quite recently, about two days or so earlier. Were they to infer that the murderous band was nearer, and might they expect to run into them at any moment?

In spite of this not very reassuring prospect, they pushed on northwards. What else could they do, anyhow? To return southwards, along a road marked out by villages hostile or destroyed, would be impossible. Better, at all costs, to reach the Niger, for there alone could they expect help.

It was so all along their route. Not a village which was not hostile, when a *tata* protected it, or, failing this, which was not pillaged, burned, devastated. Nowhere could the travellers buy food, and they existed only on chance finds : iguanas, roots unearthed in a pillaged *lougan,* lucky shots, or, sometimes, some unfortunate fish taken by St. Bérain.

This last resort, however, was seldom possible : they were now traversing country where water-courses were rare. More than once they had to suffer thirst, all the wells which they came across having been filled in. The malevolent power which strove to overwhelm them had left nothing to chance.

Yet their spirit was unbroken. Scorched by the fiery sun, dragging themselves painfully along when game was scarce, limiting their marches by their growing weakness, they still pressed on doggedly northwards, day by day, step by step, in spite of fatigue, in spite of hunger, in spite of thirst.

The two blacks faced these trials with marvellous indifference. Accustomed to privations, accustomed to poverty, they may have suffered less than their masters. They both displayed the most touching devotion.

"Me, not have much hunger." Tongané tried to persuade Malik to take an edible root he had found.

Malik accepted, only to offer the gift to Jane Blazon, who hastened to add it to the reserve which would provide the next meal for them all.

Thus each did his duty, according to his personal temperament.

Barsac's weakness was to get angry. He hardly ever spoke, and if sometimes a word escaped his lips it was mostly addressed to the French Government whose ineptitude had placed him, Barsac, in such a predicament. He could already see himself at the tribune of the Chamber, and meantime he had prepared his thunderbolts which he meant to hurl, like Jupiter, from the height of that Parliamentary Olympus.

Dr. Châtonnay similarly spoke little, but though unskilled at hunting, he was none the less useful. He searched for edible plants, and found them fairly often; and, anxious above all to keep up at least an air of cheerfulness, he never failed to laugh, with his usual sound like escaping steam, at the slightest word of Amédée Florence.

"What a pity," the latter told him, "that all you've got is a gas-leak. You haven't got a motor on you, I suppose? That would do our job for us."

At this the worthy doctor laughed once more, on principle.

M. Poncin spoke still less, because he never opened his mouth. He did not hunt, he did not fish; but on the other hand he did not complain. He did nothing, this M. Poncin, except to write now and then in his mysterious note-book; this always intrigued Amédée Florence greatly.

St. Bérain behaved as usual, neither more nor less cheerful than when they had set out. Perhaps he did not realize where he was, and was so absent-minded he did not even know when he was hungry.

To judge by appearances, Jane Blazon was supporting less philosophically the hardships with which fate had smitten them, and yet these had nothing to do with her increasing sadness. Never having expected to accomplish the journey without hardship, she took with a steadfast heart the obstacles she met with. Thin, weakened by privations and endless sufferings, her energy at least remained intact, and her thoughts were still directed towards her goal.

But the nearer she approached this, the more her misgivings and anguish increased without her being able to prevent it. What response would she get from the sepulchre at Koubo? What would she learn from the enquiry she was about to begin, centred at the place where her brother fell? Would she learn anything or would she have to return with empty hands? Such questions, every day more imperious and more absorbing, wore her down.

Amédée Florence could not help noticing her sadness, and he did his best to overcome it. He was indeed the spirit of that little world, and the worse trials did not affect his unquenchable cheerfulness. He explained that they ought to thank Heaven for its fatherly beneficence, as no other mode of life would conform better to the rules of hygiene. Whatever happened, he welcomed it. Were they thirsty? Nothing was better for his impending dilation of the stomach. Were they hungry? Nothing was better for warding off the arthritis which he dreaded. Were they worn out with fatigue? In his opinion they had never slept better. And he appealed to Dr. Châtonnay, who always agreed with him, admiring the good fellow's courage and energy.

His good qualities were the greater because he felt not only the trials common to all but a further uneasiness unsuspected by his white companions. This began on the 12th of March, when, for the first time they traversed a village whose destruction seemed to have taken place only the day before. Thenceforward he felt the firm conviction that they were being watched, trailed, spied on. Yes, spies were keeping watch in the bush, he was sure of that, escorting the despairing Mission step by step, observing its distress, ready no doubt to bring to nothing the efforts of these inland castaways at the very moment when they hoped for safety.

His eye and ear continually alert, he observed much to confirm his suspicions : in the daytime, fresh traces of recent encampments, explosions only just audible, the distant galloping of horses : during the night, mutterings, rustlings, and, now and then, the movement of a dim shadow in the gloom. Keeping his observations, his reflections, and his fears from his companions so as not to increase their anxiety, he enjoined silence on Tongané, who shared his suspicions. Until the reporter felt it advisable to take his friends into his confidence, they contented themselves with keeping a sharp look-out.

Complicated by such difficulties, the journey could never be completed within the time hoped for. Only on the evening of the 23rd March did they make their last halt before Koubo. This was still about five miles away; but within less than a mile was the place where, according to Tongané they ought to find the tomb in which lay the remains of Captain George Blazon.

Next day, at dawn, they would again set out. Leaving the road, they would go to the place where the Captain's forces had been destroyed, then make for the village. If it were in better condition than the others they would get some food and rest a few days, while Jane Blazon carried out her quest. Otherwise, they would make either for Gao or for Timbuctoo or Djenné, hoping meantime to reach lands less ravaged.

It was now that Amédée Florence thought it right to disclose his suspicions to his comrades. As they rested after the day's hardships, while Malik was cooking their meagre repast on a fire of dried grass, he told them what he had noticed. It seemed clear that they could hardly make a step without its being known to enemies who, though invisible, were always present.

"I will say more," he added. "I will dare to maintain that our adversaries have been in contact with us before; they're almost old comrades. I hold to it, until I'm proved wrong, that they comprise twenty blacks and three whites, and that one of these looks like the twin of our elegant friend, the self-styled

Lieutenant Lacour, so favourably known to this honourable company."

"On what do you base this hypothesis, Monsieur Florence?" asked Barsac.

"On this: first, that our so-called escort could easily have learned our intentions and preceded us along our route and so carried out for our benefit the pretty work you've all been able to admire. It would be difficult to postulate an entirely different troop who, not knowing our plans, or even of our existence, would be acting in this way for reasons we cannot understand. There's something else, too. The inhabitants of the looted villages and that old negro whom the doctor patched up before Kadou all suffered in the same way. So the murderers must have been near us before the second escort arrived, just as they have since it left."

"You may be right, Monsieur Florence," Barsac agreed, "but you haven't told us much after all. Nobody doubts that this devastation was directed against us. Whether it's the work of Lieutenant Lacour or somebody else, whether the bandits are around us instead of simply in front of us as we thought, that doesn't alter our situation at all."

"That's not my view," replied Amédée Florence. "So much so that I decided to speak at last after keeping silence so long so as not to increase your anxiety needlessly. But now, in spite of everything, we've reached our goal. To-morrow either we shall be at Koubo, and so in safety, or else our direction will change and perhaps they'll stop persecuting us. I want, I don't mind saying, to deceive the spies for once, so that nobody will know what we're going to do."

"With what aim?" asked Barsac.

"I'm not too certain about it," Florence declared. "It's just an idea of mine. But it seems better to me, in Miss Blazon's interests, that the direction we're taking should not be known until her enquiries are complete."

"I quite agree with Monsieur Florence," Jane Blazon concurred. "Who knows whether our adversaries may not be about to declare war against us openly? Perhaps it will be to-morrow they'll attack us, to sink us just as we get into harbour. But I don't want to come so far without completing my quest. That's why I think Monsieur Florence is right in wanting to escape from the spies around us. Unfortunately I can't see how!"

"Nothing easier to my mind," Florence explained. "So far, at any rate, they haven't risked a direct attack. They've been content to hinder our progress and spy on us, and if Miss Blazon is right they won't interfere directly until our obstinacy gets the better of their patience. Probably their watchfulness relaxes when they feel certain we've settled down for the night. Our regular routine must reassure them, and they'll never doubt that they'll find us in the morning where they left us at nightfall.

"There's no reason why they should be more vigilant to-day than any other day, unless they've decided to attack us forthwith. If they have, it will be more necessary than ever to try to go off at a tangent. But if not, nothing can be easier than to set out at once, taking advantage of the darkness. We'll go one by one, making as little noise as possible, aiming for a general rendezvous. After all, it isn't a countless host we've got to deal with, and it would be sheer bad luck if we were to fall over the seductive Lieutenant Lacour."

Jane Blazon heartily approved, and it was settled that one after another they should go eastwards towards a large clump of trees which they had noticed at nightfall about a mile away. The trees were now invisible, but they could make certain of reaching them by taking their direction from a star twinkling on the horizon above the thick clouds which added to the darkness. Tongané would go first, then Jane Blazon, then Malik; the others would follow in succession, with Amédée Florence as rearguard.

Their departure took place without incident. Two hours later they were reunited on the edge of the clump of trees. They hurried through them, so as to place that impenetrable screen between themselves and the enemy. Then they advanced more quickly. To be so near their goal gave them new heart, and none of them felt tired.

After half an hour's quick walk, Tongané paused. He thought they were near the very spot where the rebel Captain's forces had been exterminated; but in the darkness he could not pick out exactly the place which Jane Blazon sought. They would have to wait for the day.

They then took several hours' rest. Jane Blazon, not knowing what the next dawn would reveal, was the only one unable to sleep. More pressing than before, a hundred questions thronged into her mind. Was her ill-fated brother really dead, and could she find evidence not destroyed by time? If such evidence existed, would it tend to confirm his guilt, or would it prove his innocence, or would it leave them still in doubt? And to-morrow, where was she to begin the enquiry she was determined to make? Might not the last witnesses of the tragedy have scattered, vanished, perhaps died themselves? Or could she find any of them? If she succeeded, what would be the truth she would learn from their mouth?

A little before six they were all ready. Until the day broke they waited, gripped by a strong emotion, their eyes fixed on Tongané, who was examining his surroundings and looking for some landmark.

"There!" he said at last, pointing towards a tree standing by itself on the plain three or four hundred yards away.

A little later they were all at its foot. As Tongané was still quite certain, they attacked the ground where he pointed out, though there was nothing to indicate the presence of a grave. Feverishly they hacked up the soil with their knives, throwing it by handfuls on the sides of the rapidly deepening excavation.

"Look out!" the reporter cried suddenly. "Here are some bones. . . ."

Deeply moved, Miss Blazon had to lean on the doctor's arm.

Carefully they at last uncovered the remains: a body, or

rather a skeleton in a marvellous state of preservation. On what had once been the arms were fragments of material and some gold embroidery, indicative of rank. Among the bones of the chest they found a wallet, almost completely destroyed by the weather. They opened it. It contained only one document; a letter to George Blazon from his sister.

Tears gushed from the young girl's eyes. She raised to her lips the discoloured paper, which crumbled between her fingers; then, half fainting, she approached the grave.

"Doctor," she said to Châtonnay in a trembling voice. "Please, won't you be good enough to investigate my poor brother's remains?"

"At your service, Miss Blazon," replied the doctor, so distressed that he almost forgot the hunger gnawing at his vitals.

He got down into the grave and began, with the care and precision of a police-surgeon, to make the examination. When he had finished, his face was very serious and showed an intense emotion.

"I, Laurent Châtonnay, Doctor of Medicine of the University of Paris," he said, not without a certain solemnity, and in the midst of a profound silence, "I certify as follows: First, the bones presented to me for examination, and which Miss Jane Blazon declares to be those of her brother George Blazon, show no trace of a wound made with firearms; secondly, the man from whom these bones came has been murdered; thirdly, that death was the result of a dagger-thrust delivered downwards, which broke through the left shoulder-blade and reached one of the upper lobes of the heart; fourthly, that this is the weapon, withdrawn by my hand from the bony sheath in which it was still embedded."

"Murdered!" whispered Jane, overcome.

"Murdered, I assert," repeated Dr. Châtonnay.

"And from behind!"

"From behind."

"Then George must be innocent!" cried Jane Blazon, bursting into sobs.

"The innocence of your brother is a question beyond my purview, Miss Blazon," replied Doctor Châtonnay gently, "and I cannot assert it with the same assurance as the material facts which I have adduced, but I must tell you I think it infinitely probable. The result of my examination, indeed, is that your brother did not fall weapons in hand, as has hitherto been thought, but that he was struck down from behind, before, during, or after, the salvo which has been recorded. When exactly, and by whom, was he struck? I do not know. All that one can say is that the blow was not delivered by regular troops, for the weapon which slew your brother is not a military weapon but a dagger."

"Thank you, Doctor," said Jane, who was gradually recovering her self-control. "The first results of our journey, at any rate, have given me confidence. One thing more, Doctor: would you be willing to set down in writing what you have seen to-day, and would these gentlemen be kind enough to act as witnesses?"

They willingly hastened to carry out Jane Blazon's request. On a sheet which M. Poncin agreed to detach from his note-book, Amédée Florence set out the facts. Then this attestation, signed by Dr. Châtonnay and witnessed by everyone present, was given to Jane Blazon with the weapon found in her brother's grave.

The young girl trembled as she touched this. It was a dagger, thickly coated with rust, perhaps mixed with blood. On the ebony handle, half decayed in the damp ground, they could still make out the trace of some obliterated lettering.

"Look at this, gentlemen," said Jane, showing them these almost invisible markings, "this weapon is marked with the murderer's name."

"A pity it's effaced," sighed Amédée Florence, as he examined the dagger. "But wait a minute. . . . I can make out something . . . an 'i' and an 'l', I think."

"That's not much," said Barsac.

THE FOREST GRAVE

"Perhaps we shan't need any more to unmask the assassin," Jane said gravely.

At her request Tongané carefully replaced the earth over the remains of George Blazon, Then, leaving the tragic grave in its loneliness, they made for Koubo.

But after two or three miles they had to halt. Strength failed Jane Blazon; her knees gave way beneath her, and she sank to the ground.

"Emotion," explained Dr. Châtonnay.

"And hunger," added Amédée Florence quite accurately. "Come along, old St. Bérain, are you going to watch your niece die of hunger, even though she's your aunt, devil take it! Go and hunt! And mind you don't mistake me for the game!"

Unfortunately game was scarce. Most of the day elapsed before the two hunters found anything at the muzzles of their rifles, but at last fortune favoured them. Indeed, things had never been so good, two bustards and a partridge falling, one after another, to their shots. For the first time for days they could have a good meal. So they decided not to try to reach Koubo that evening, but to spend a last night in the open air.

Worn out with fatigue, and convinced that they had thrown their enemies off the track, the travellers neglected the watch they had hitherto kept. So none of them saw some strange phenomena which appeared during the night. Westwards, faint lights flickered here and there on the plain.

Brighter lights replied to them in the east; although there were no mountains in that unusually flat country, these lights were high above the ground. Little by little the feeble gleams in the west and the powerful lights in the east approached each other, the former slowly, the latter more quickly. All converged on the point where the sleepers lay.

Suddenly these were awakened brusquely by the strange roaring sound which they had already heard near Kankan. Now, however, it was much nearer and much more intense. Scarcely had they opened their eyes when dazzling beams, glaring from about ten centres of brilliance like searchlights, flared out suddenly to the east of them, less than a hundred yards away. They were trying to understand this when some men, emerging from the shadows, entered the cone of light and leapt on the startled and half-blinded sleepers. In an instant these were hurled to the ground.

Out of the darkness beyond, a brutal voice asked in French: "Are you there, boys?"

Then, after a brief silence: "The first to move will get a bullet in his head. Come on, you there, let's get going!"